LONE WOLF

LONE WOLF

Kristine L. Franklin

SCHOLASTIC INC.

New York Toronto London Auckland Sydney

ISBN 0-590-55105-1

12 11 10 9 8 7 6 5 4 3 2   9/9 0 1 2 3/0

Printed in the U.S.A.   40

First Scholastic printing, January, 1998

This book was typeset in New Baskerville.

For J. O.

Amicus et frater sine pare.

CHAPTER

1

Just before I came inside and started the fire, I stood and watched the old white house. It looks like it's sleeping. All the drapes are shut tight, to keep out the cold, and there's a blanket hanging up to cover the window in Ian and Katie's room. The dogs are inside; the car is put away. If it weren't for that white curl of smoke twisting up from the chimney, and all the sleds and junk scattered around the yard, you wouldn't know there's a bunch of people living there. You wouldn't know the TV is blasting and a couple kids are fighting, and a mom is yelling, and an artist dad is figuring out how to draw a mushroom or an oak tree so it looks alive.

From the outside, it's a silent house, snoozing between the bare white birch trees. Inside, it's a commotion. Guaranteed. And it's as warm as July. That house is always warm and noisy, now that it's full.

It's warm in here, too. Almost too warm. Today is the thirty-first of December and it's ten below zero outside. It'll get even colder before springtime comes. It'll be months before the snow melts and the willows up at Howling Lake get their baby leaves. It's amazing how warm this place can be when outside it's cold enough to freeze your lips off. Good thing I've got a fresh supply of firewood. I don't know how long I'll be here. I brought a little reading project that might take me a while to finish.

I found this cave the first time I went hiking after Dad and I moved up here to the north woods from St. Paul. That'll be three years next June. The cave is up high on the side of a steep hill with a ledge out in front, where you can walk. It's the coolest hideout in the world. I practically missed it the first time because the entrance is super narrow at the top and hidden between these two giant hunks of granite. You have to squeeze sideways to get inside. The cave goes back about fifteen feet, and for more than half that length even a tall grownup can stand up straight. If I sit at just the right angle, I can barely see the old white house from here.

The first time I saw that house it was summer and all the trees had leaves, so the only thing I could see was the chimney. I scrambled down the hill to take a closer look, hoping there might be a boy my age to play with. All I found was the empty house with its ugly peeling paint and a dirty For Sale sign in one window and a crooked wooden sign on the porch that said THE BENNETTS. For a long time, I called it the Bennett House. Once I got up the nerve to try the doors but they were all locked. After that I stayed away, partly because Dad taught me not to trespass, and partly because empty houses are full of spooky noises that can make your hands itch with sweat.

That first summer I kept hoping another boy would move into that house, someone my age, someone to hang around and do stuff with. I had Rhonda, and she's good as far as dogs go, but dogs aren't the same as people. That first summer I missed Billy Zimmerman and Alec Rodale, my neighbors from before. I thought at least when I started school I'd make some new friends, but then Dad told me he wanted me to do home school and I missed my friends even more. I missed seeing Grandma every Sunday, and my aunt Stephie when she came home from college to do her laundry. It didn't seem fair to have to move way up here where there weren't any other kids. I'd never heard of kids doing school at home and at first I didn't like the idea. But I never told Dad I felt that way because I was scared it would only make him mad to know. He might think I was complaining about his decision to live in the woods, away from civilization. My dad hates complaining. It's one of the things he and Mom fought about. If Mom even said one thing about how Dad did something, he got mad. So I knew it wouldn't do any good to tell him I was missing my friends. I knew there was no turning back. When my dad makes up his mind about something, that's that. I knew that when I chose to go with him.

I didn't know Mom left us until Dad told me. It was night, and I was asleep. Dad came into my room and shook me awake. He said, "Your mother is leaving and she's not coming back." At first I thought he meant she was leaving to go to the store or to Grandma's, but when he said I'd have to choose, him or her, it was like he'd poured cold water on my head. Mom or Dad. How could I choose? It's not like I had a lot of time to think it over. Dad sat on the side of my bed and stared down at me. His eyes were like black empty holes. I swallowed down the terrible taste in my mouth.

"You" was all I could say. He nodded and said OK. I squeezed my eyes shut so he wouldn't see the tears. I didn't want him to think I was sorry about choosing him. When I looked again, he was gone. Mom was gone too; gone for good, Dad said. She didn't want me and Dad anymore.

That's why I chose Dad. Mom never came to ask me who I wanted. She just left without even saying good-bye. Dad let me choose. The next week Dad and I moved up here. He didn't mention my mom at all the whole week we were getting ready. That was back when I was eight.

Dad said up here we would be able to forget everything that had happened and start a new life on our own, just me and him. Boy, did I ever want to forget! And I wanted to be strong like Dad, to never feel lonely, to never miss anyone. My dad is good at being strong. But still, I was only a little kid when we came, and sometimes in my cave, when I was by myself, a whole bunch of bad feelings would swell my throat up and choke me until I could hardly breathe. It took a ton of willpower not to cry. I thought about how tough my dad is. I tried to be like him. It took a lot of practice. After a while, it worked. After a while, I could think about my mom leaving us, about everything else that had happened before, and not feel a thing.

I've never seen Dad cry. Not even the day my sister died. He came and got me out of school and the thing I remember most is that his face was as white as a piece of paper. Seriously. His dark eyes were small and hard and even though he looked at me, it seemed he was looking at something far away. That look terrified me. Then when he said, "Mom was in a car accident," I wanted to plug my ears so I couldn't hear any more. Dad took a big gulp of air. "Mom's fine," he said in a whisper. "But Olivia . . . your little sis—" He didn't finish the sentence. He looked away, his arms folded tightly across his chest. I just stood there. I knew she was dead, even though he didn't say the word, even though I was just a little first grader who didn't know too much. He's never said it. Dead that is.

We walked out to the car and went to the hospital where Mom was, but I hardly remember any of that. It was like everything went small in my mind. Things got real, real far away; noises were tiny. Even Mom's crying and hugging me from her hospital bed, and her two black eyes. It was all like it was happening on TV.

From then on, I erased things out of my mind as soon as they happened. All the relatives hugging and squeezing me. Grandma crying, her tears dripping on my cheek. The funeral and the priest in his long white robe and the smell of the incense smoke mixed with the smell of burning candles and lots and lots of flowers. The hole in the ground where they put the casket. The blue velvet seats inside the big funeral car we rode in. Mom with her black eyes, crying, sniffling, shaking all the time. All the food, all the phone calls. All the sad-looking, blubbering people. I wanted it to be happening to someone else, some other boy. I wanted to erase every smell and sight and sound from my brain. I kept my eyes on my dad. He was so strong. I wanted to be just like him.

After the accident, Mom cried all the time. Some days she didn't get dressed. Grandma was over a lot. Why couldn't Mom be strong too? Why couldn't she be like Dad and me? When she cried I wanted to do something to make her stop. At first I tried to hug her, but she'd hug me for a second and then push me away and cry even harder. Other times I got so mad about all her crying that I wanted to scream and hit her and make her shut up. I think Dad must have felt the same way, because they started fighting every time Mom cried. They'd always fought a lot before, but now it was worse. It got so bad that whenever they started to yell at each other, I crawled under my bed and pretended it was a cave. I pretended I was a cave boy who hunted animals for food. Once when Mom was really screaming at Dad, I took a pencil and drew caveman drawings under my bed on the wall. When Mom found the drawings, I got a spanking.

A whole year went by after the accident. My mom got worse. One day she got a bunch of those big black garbage bags and filled them with my sister's things. She took everything, clothes, toys, even the little sheets that go on the crib. She tore the *Sesame Street* wallpaper off the walls in long strips. When she was done, my sister's room was bare. When my dad came home he had a fit. They fought way into the night. I crawled under my bed like usual and put a pillow over my head. I woke up there the next morning.

My dad got quieter than ever before after that. When Mom and Dad weren't fighting they didn't talk to each other. I stayed out of their way. I didn't make any trouble. I didn't cry once. It felt good to act strong, even stronger than a grownup like my mom.

I was in second grade when Mom left. Then we moved here.

Beavers nibble all the bark off a birch twig and leave the white wood behind. A stick with all the bark off, a natural one with beaver teeth marks on it, is called a beaver stick. They're really cool to find. Right after we moved here, I figured out that if I picked at a twig with my fingernails I could make my own white stick. It took a long time to get all the bark off, but it hurt so much that for a while I could forget about the other stuff, the stuff that made me feel like I might cry any minute, just like a big baby. So whenever I would get those weakling feelings, like missing my friends or family, I'd get out one of my sticks and start picking. Crying is for wimps. That's what I told myself, sometimes a hundred times a day. Concentrating on the beaver stick helped. Sometimes my fingernails actually bled, but it was worth it. I made four white sticks that way, all by hand. I kept them right up until a month ago.

Sometimes while I was working on the beaver sticks I'd sit out on the ledge and look down at the Bennett House. Month after month it sat empty and alone. Sometimes I imagined the windows were eyes, staring out at the forest, at nothing. An empty old house doesn't think about anything, I thought. What would that be like? I finished the sticks and after a while the months turned into a couple of years and I stopped hoping anyone would move in. I came to my cave almost every day, as long as it wasn't too cold. I drew pictures on the walls inside. I built a fire ring at the entrance and pulled a big rock in to sit on.

After a while, instead of picking at sticks and wishing we could move back to St. Paul, I started noticing all the different kinds of birds that came around, and pretty soon I knew which ones made which songs. I invented a game. I would sit outside my cave and listen to the sounds with my eyes shut, I mean really *listen*. Then I would open my eyes and try to find what animal or bird had made the sound. Sometimes I had to hike around to find it, like a wild boy hunting for his food.

I learned the pips and chitters of squirrels and chipmunks and the hammering sound the woodpecker makes. I learned a ton of birdcalls. I can even imitate some of the sounds. Sometimes the birds answer back, especially owls.

Then one day a few months ago, around the first

of September, I thought I heard a new bird sound, a different kind of owl maybe, so I closed my eyes and listened real hard, only to hear this yipping and then a long pitiful howl. No way was it a bird. I knew what it was from this tape I have of wild-animal sounds. It was a wolf. I was positive about it. There are a few timber wolves up here, but they're so scared of people you hardly ever see them. Hearing a wolf, a real live wolf, was a huge thrill.

Even though I didn't see the wolf, I gave it a name. King. I knew it just had to be gigantic, maybe a hundred pounds or so, and strong and free, the king of the north woods. He was probably a lone wolf, one who goes off by himself away from the other wolves to wander until he finds a mate and starts his own pack. That's the way I imagined it, anyway.

About three days later I was up here hoping I'd hear King again, when this big truck came grinding and rumbling up the overgrown dirt-track driveway. I heard its brakes squeal when it stopped beside the Bennett House. The leaves were still on the trees then, so I couldn't see what was going on. I threw some dirt on my little campfire and scrambled down the hill to get a closer look. In all the times I'd been to my cave, I'd never once heard a car come up that road.

CHAPTER
2

I got as far as the old shed at the back of the property and crouched behind it to watch. Good thing Rhonda was home with a sore foot. She would have given me away in a second. OK, maybe I *was* trespassing, but sometimes a guy doesn't have a choice. A big orange U-Haul van was parked beside the house. A beat-up old station wagon pulled up behind, and when it stopped, the first one out was the driver, a tall woman with carrot orange hair. She said something into the car, then she went around to the passenger side and opened the door. She reached inside and brought out a little kid. He was bigger than a baby, but he had that big rear end that means one thing. Diapers.

My hands were itching like crazy. Trespassing has that effect on a person. Just then both back-seat doors opened up. A skinny girl with long, droopy black hair and big glasses got out and looked around. Skinny is not the right word. She was a total toothpick. I didn't know humans came so skinny. I ducked behind the shed when she looked in my direction.

Another girl got out, a little smaller than the first one. Her hair was dark and cut short. She had glasses too. Then another girl got out. She was sort of chubby with brown hair in really messy ponytails. Glasses. I couldn't see who got out on the other side. I held my breath. It *had* to be a boy.

A little girl, a redheaded one with red glasses, ran up the steps. Now they were all talking and bouncing around and yelling. Two black ragged-looking small dogs jumped out of the car and started yipping. A tiger cat stepped delicately down and sniffed the air. No other people. Only a whole herd of girls with glasses, and a baby.

No boys.

I stayed long enough to watch a thin guy with curly gray hair and a big guy with a blond beard carry a red couch inside; long enough to know it was for sure that there weren't any boys, except the baby, who didn't count. Then I walked home the long way, kicking every mushroom I could find until they looked like white smears in the dirt.

When I got home Dad was sitting at the kitchen table. He looked up when I came in, but he didn't say anything. The table was spread with papers and he had his calculator and the checkbook out. Dad doesn't like to be interrupted when he's doing bills, but I thought he ought to know about the new neighbors. I told him about seeing the skinny girl and her sisters. He nodded and smoothed his mustache with two fingers. "Nothing wrong with girls," said Dad. I made a gagging noise. Dad shrugged and stood up. Then he said, "I've got some wood to chop," and went outside.

As soon as the door shut behind him, I had a punched feeling in my gut. Dad doesn't like to talk much. I knew that. And he doesn't like to listen to talking either. I should have been used to it by now. So why did it bug me so much that he'd walked out? I went to the fridge and pulled out a carton of milk. As long as the new neighbors were too far away to see or hear, Dad wouldn't think twice about them. I wished I could do the same.

The problem was I was worried sick about all those girls being practically on top of my private cave. They'd find me and ruin my peace and quiet with all their giggling and stupid goofing off. They'd make a dollhouse out of my cave, and then maybe they'd want to play store and school! For sure they'd scare all the birds away, and probably once King got a whiff of them, he'd stay far away, too.

I hadn't been around other kids for a long time, not since Dad and I came up here to live by ourselves, but I knew one thing: I wasn't so desperate for friends that I'd hang out with a bunch of little smelly squealy girls. During dinner, I was still thinking about them. I wanted to tell Dad I was worried about them taking over my cave, but I figured he wouldn't care too much, so I didn't mention it. He knew about the cave, and he knew I went to it all the time, but he never asked me any questions about it; and I never talked about it. That's just the way we are. After dinner, while Dad finished paying the bills, instead of reading, like I usually do, I turned on the television and watched three hours of stupid programs. The satellite dish was here when we moved in. I don't think Dad would have bought one. We get a million channels, mostly boring stuff. That night it was double boring, a total waste of time. When I went to bed, I was still thinking about those girls. The really skinny one looked about my age. How could my luck be so rotten?

CHAPTER
3

The day after the new people moved in I got up before dawn. I had a lot of work to do. I'd been so bummed out about all those girls that I hadn't stopped to think that maybe I could protect my cave from discovery. Now I was in a big hurry. I had to get to my cave, hide all my firewood inside, and camouflage the entrance in case anyone came snooping around. I'd realized the night before, lying awake in bed and thinking about it, that soon all those girls would be in school all day and I could go to my cave whenever I wanted, except maybe for weekends. All I had to do was protect it from possible weekend snooping. Piece of cake! I fed Rhonda, fixed myself some microwave oatmeal, and we took off.

Rhonda ran ahead on the trail, still limping a bit. She'd been in the house for days after getting a porcupine quill stuck in her paw, and I felt sorry for her being cooped up like that. German shepherds need a lot of exercise. It was so early, barely dawn, that I wasn't worried about her giving us away. Those new people were probably city people, the kind that get up at nine or ten on Saturdays. Just thinking about them invading my territory made me mad. Feeling mad gave me plenty of energy to work.

It took me more than an hour to move my woodpile from outside to inside the cave. I stacked the wood in the back of the cave, fitting all the pieces together carefully so I could store as much as possible and not worry about the whole stack falling over. When I was done I went outside and looked toward the Bennett House. It wasn't fair that they were all girls. It just wasn't fair. Maybe they'd be too scared to go snooping around in the woods.

The wind had picked up and it felt like the temperature was dropping. September can be a tricky month. Some days are like summer, hot and sticky and still, with thunderstorms in the afternoon. Then all of a sudden, there is a hard frost, just like that, and all the mushrooms turn to slime, the leaves fall off the trees, the flowers die. It felt like a cold front was coming our way, maybe the first killing frost. I shivered and looked at my watch. Quarter to eight. They wouldn't be up for hours. I had on only a zip-up sweatshirt and the wind went right through it. I had plenty of time to make a little fire and get warmed up while I figured out how to hide the entrance.

The first time I had made a campfire in the cave I was nervous. In fact, I lit the fire pretty close to the entrance and waited outside to see if smoke filled the cave. What I found out was that the narrow top of the entrance is at just the right angle to pull the smoke out as it collects at the top of the cave. When I went inside, I couldn't smell a speck of smoke and after that I made fires whenever it was cold. Of course, back then, when it got too cold, way below zero, for instance, even the campfire wasn't warm enough and I had to stay home. I hated those cold, boring days.

Rhonda flopped down beside the ring of stones that was my campfire and licked her sore paw. I got the fire going and warmed my hands in its glow. I thought about covering the entrance to the cave. Maybe I could stack a bunch of rocks. Or maybe I could pile some brush. My goal was to make it so that if any of those girls walked by, they wouldn't notice the cave entrance. At the same time, I had to figure out how to do it so I could still get in when I wanted to without a lot of hassle. If I covered the entrance with big rocks, I'd have to move them. Brush seemed like a better idea. I could find some old branches, stumps, maybe add some fresh stuff. It seemed like a good idea. By then I was warmed up and ready to get back to work.

Suddenly Rhonda's head shot up. Her black ears stood straight up. I listened until I could hear what she was hearing. "*Tunafish!*" called a faraway voice. "*Here, Tuna!*" I jumped up and looked out. I didn't see anything. "*Here, kitty kitty!*" The voice was closer now, coming up the hill toward my camp. It had to be one of those girls!

I rushed over to the campfire. Could she smell the smoke? I looked out. There was almost no smoke but I could still smell the burning wood.

"*Tunafish!*"

Rhonda whined and stood up. "Down!" I told her. She dropped. Good thing she's just about the world's best-trained dog. My heart raced, and so did my brain. If I dumped dirt on the fire, like I usually do to put it out, it would make tons of smoke. So that was no good. I couldn't leave either, not with the fire going. At least the firewood was stacked inside. Maybe she wouldn't see the entrance. Chances are she won't, I thought. Chances are she'll never even get close.

The girl called and called. I wondered which one it was. Skinny? Short hair? Pudgy? It couldn't be the redheaded one. She was way too little to be wandering around in the woods. Whoever she was, she came closer. *"Tunafish! Where are you?"* she called, and I thought it was the stupidest name for a cat I'd ever heard. I was barely breathing. I stared at Rhonda so she wouldn't whine. She looked at me and begged with her eyes. She knows what "kitty kitty" means. She's not dense. She wanted to go out and find that cat, too. *"Tuna!"* called the voice, this time a little desperate sounding and a lot closer than the last time.

I looked up and willed the slight wisp of smoke to blow away in the breeze, away, away from that *girl,* whichever one she was, wherever she was. Thank goodness it was getting windy. Rhonda whined again. I whirled around to shut her up. She was staring at the entrance to my cave and her ears were twitching. I looked and watched with horror as a fluffy orange cat tiptoed into my cave.

CHAPTER
4

Rhonda whine-growled. That's what she does when she's super excited and doesn't want to stay. "Quiet!" I told her. The cat stopped and looked at us then took a couple steps closer. Rhonda thumped her tail. She adores cats. *"Pssst!"* I hissed at the cat. *"Get out. Shoo."*

Don't get me wrong. It's not that I hate cats or anything. I'd have one if Dad weren't allergic. It's just that there was no way I wanted *that* cat in my personal cave, especially with a girl out looking for it, getting closer by the second.

The orange cat ignored me and made a beeline to Rhonda, who was now swishing her tail so hard it made a dirt cloud. Any other dog would have been jumping all over the place. Not Rhonda. When I tell her to stay, she stays, unless it's an emergency.

"Here, kitty kitty."

She was practically outside the door! I wanted to scoop the cat up and toss it outside. Rhonda whined again. The cat walked over and rubbed against her shoulder. The dirt cloud got worse. Rhonda whimpered. "Meow?" asked the cat.

"Knock it *off,*" I whispered, but they didn't pay any attention to me. I grabbed the cat. "Quiet, Rhonda," I said in my sternest whisper.

"YOW!" cried the cat, and it kicked at my stomach with its back legs. Sharp claws dug right through my sweatshirt and I dropped the cat on Rhonda's head. Rhonda yipped and jumped up as the cat's claws dug into her face. The cat fell into the dirt, hunched its back and hissed, then ran to the back of the cave.

"*Down!*" I said to Rhonda. She dropped to the ground, but not before she barked two times at that stupid cat.

"Tuna? Are you in there?" The voice was right outside. I bit my lip and frowned at Rhonda. Then the cat started up.

"Yow, yow, yow," it cried. I heard a gasp outside.

"Tuna! Oh, my baby kitty! Come out! *Come out!*"

I swallowed. I tried to reach the cat with my foot to shove it toward the entrance, but it was out of my reach. I was too scared to go after it, too scared of making noise.

"YOW, YOW, YOW."

I was trapped. She'd found me. I stood there waiting for her to rush in and rescue her idiotic cat, but nothing happened. In fact, I listened hard and didn't hear a thing. It felt like an hour had passed while I stood there expecting her to come barging in. Pretty soon the cat started cleaning itself. This is ridiculous, I thought. My stomach was balled up, my heart was pumping in my ears, my hands were itchy, I was furious at Rhonda for barking, and I wasn't going to wait for any girl.

I took a deep breath and squeezed out the entrance. I didn't see anyone. I peeked around the rock and *WHOOSH!* a huge branch swung past my nose and almost knocked my brains out. I heard a scream. I jumped back and whacked my head. I scrunched my eyes shut in agony and when I opened them, there was Skinny, staring at me through her big glasses, with a huge birch log in her hands.

"I thought you were a mountain lion!" she yelled. Her voice was shaking.

"You almost killed me!" I shouted. I rubbed the back of my head. "Do I look like a mountain lion?"

"No, but how was I supposed to know there was a boy in there?" She tossed the stick down and put her hands on her hips. She was breathing hard. "I heard my poor cat crying inside and then I heard growling and hissing and thought it was a wild animal. Didn't you hear me?"

"I heard you," I said.

"So why didn't you call me and let me know you weren't a bear or a lion? Why did you kidnap my poor cat and trap her in there?"

"I didn't kidnap your cat. Why don't you keep your stupid cat at home?"

"You're changing the subject," she snapped.

"You're *trespassing*," I shouted.

"My mom and dad bought all this land with our house." She stuck out her bony chin at me and squinted her eyes. " *You're* trespassing." My stomach dropped down to my knees. *No!* Could it be true? Could my cave, my wonderful secret hideout, my privacy place, be part of the Bennett House property? That possibility had never occured to me before. I opened my mouth to shout back at her.

"Oh" was all that came out. We stood there and stared at each other. Her eyes were so dark I could hardly see the pupils. She frowned at me through her glasses. A strand of her long, stringy hair hung in her face. Who knows what she thought of the brown-haired regular-looking eleven-year-old kid she saw staring at her like a total moron. All *I* could see was an ugly, skinny girl. She was the enemy, and now she was taking away the best place I'd ever called my own.

"Where's my cat?"

"Inside," I said, stepping aside so she could squeeze past me into the cave. "My dog's in there, too. She won't hurt you." I shut my eyes and leaned back against the cold rock. I was defeated. My eyes felt hot and my nose burned and I wanted to pound something. It was my own stupid fault for not hiding the entrance sooner. It was my own fault!

"Hey!" called the girl. "Come in here a second." I sighed and went inside. I bit the inside of my cheek as I looked around my cave, or rather, *her* cave. The thought of it felt like a pain in my gut. I knew I couldn't keep coming here. You can't just use someone else's property without permission. I wasn't about to ask for permission, either. Rhonda was still in the down-stay. I patted my leg and she leaped toward me.

"Let's go, Rhonda," I said and started to leave.

"You don't have to go," said the girl. She had the cat in her arms and she didn't look mad anymore. She looked around. "Whew," she said. "You really scared me. Is this your secret hideout?" She stood in the place where the light comes in. She had to squint to see me because I was in the shadows.

"It was. It's not a secret anymore, though, is it?" I didn't look at her. The thief. The enemy. That's all I could think of, even though the cave was on her property. I scratched Rhonda's back.

"Your dog is really pretty," said the girl. I didn't say anything. "She's a German shepherd, huh?"

I didn't answer. I looked at the firewood I'd hauled and stacked, enough for a couple months. My white sticks were behind them. Now I'd never get to make anything with them. All that work for nothing. The inside of my cheek hurt from biting it. "Outside," I said to Rhonda. She shot out the door and waited for me.

"How come your dog is limping?" asked the girl.

"Porcupine quill," I said. I turned my back on her. This was it. The last time I'd ever see my cave. All that time I'd wished for another kid to play with, a boy, and this is what I got. I had to get out of there. I couldn't stand being around her for another second.

"It could still be your cave," said the girl. "I won't tell. I swear."

"Forget it," I said. First she's trying to kill me with a branch, I thought, then she's yelling at me, then she's all nice and acting friendly. I didn't trust her. Half of me wanted to leave right then and there, show her I couldn't care less about the cave, even if I *had* spent the last two and a half years of my life hanging out in it. The other half of me couldn't bear to leave it. I drew a circle in the dirt with my toe. Skinny came around and looked at me.

"Do you live around here?" she asked.

I nodded.

"I didn't think we had any neighbors. We could share the cave," she said. "It's really cool. I've never been in a cave before." I frowned at her and her words came out in a flood. "Maybe I could just come once in a while, and I'd promise never to mess anything up. See, there're so many kids in my family and I've always wished for a place I could get away from them and be all alone, all by myself or maybe with one other person, *not* one of my sisters, though, and Ian's too little for anything—" She stopped talking and stared through those glasses at me. "We could have, you know, joint ownership."

No way. I could never share my cave. "It's on your property," I said. "I'm not coming here anymore." It was all mine or I didn't want anything to do with it. As long as only I knew about it, it was a secret, a special place. So what if she swore she'd never tell. Girls are blabbermouths, I thought. Just listen to this one! Jeez. Diarrhea mouth is more like it. Next thing I knew my personal hideaway would be full of Barbie dolls. No. *No way.* I gritted my teeth together, but still, I couldn't make myself leave.

Just then, the girl looked up and noticed the walls and ceiling of my cave and her mouth dropped open. She took a step in so she could see better and look some more. "Wow!" she said. Then she grinned at me. It was a goofy, crooked smile. Her mouth tilted up toward the left and her two big front teeth kind of hung out beaverlike. "You're a great artist!" she said. I felt my face turn red.

"No, I'm not."

She walked over to the cave wall and touched the stone. With her finger, she outlined a buffalo picture I'd drawn with a piece of charcoal.

"I copied them from a library book."

"They're perfect," she said. "Just like the real thing." Now she was looking at the horse drawings.

There were guys with spears, deer, dogs, moose too. I'd decorated all the walls and the ceiling as far up as I could reach. I'd never in a million years expected another person to see them.

"Thanks," I said.

"I promise promise *promise* not to tell anyone," she said and looked at me with that same look Rhonda gets when she wants a potato chip. "I'm an artist too," she added. She looked at me like she expected me to say something. I kept quiet. Did I care if she thought she was an artist? Who ever heard of a kid artist?

"I bet there aren't any other kids around here," she said.

"That's right," I said. "Not until you get about five miles from Grand Marais."

"So don't stay away, okay?"

"I don't know," I said and whistled for Rhonda. The thought of giving up my cave forever was starting to sink in. Maybe one other person knowing wasn't such a disaster. Rhonda came in and sat at my left side. "Promise not to tell anyone else? I mean it."

Skinny crossed her heart. "I swear," she said, and grinned even harder than before.

CHAPTER
5

What's your name, anyway?" I asked without looking at her. I dragged my big rock over next to the
fire and sat down. Maybe she wouldn't come to the
cave that much, I thought. Maybe she'd get tired of
it. She was still admiring my cave pictures.

"Willow Anne-Marie Pestalozzi," she said. She sat
down on my regular sitting stump, the cat draped
across her arms.

"Big name," I said. "Is that Italian?"

"Duh." She rolled her eyes. "What's yours?"

"Perry Dubois," I said.

"I bet that's French." I felt like saying "Duh," but
I didn't.

"French-Canadian. My great-grandpa came from
Montreal."

"Then you're supposed to say Du-BWAH," said

Willow. "Not Du-BOICE." I felt my face turn red. The last thing I needed was a know-it-all girl telling me how to pronounce my own name.

"We say it American-style." Like I should have to explain.

Willow raised her eyebrows once and nodded.

I could hear the cat purr. "Pass me some firewood, would ya?" I said. She reached back and grabbed a piece off the pile.

"Should I put it on the fire?" She held the wood over the fire but didn't drop it.

"Yeah." She dropped the wood and it sent up a spray of sparks. The wood caught fire and I warmed my hands over the new flame. It felt really strange to be in my cave with another person. I was having second thoughts about the joint ownership thing. Why hadn't I followed my instinct when I'd first heard her calling her idiotic cat? Why hadn't I run as fast as I could in the opposite direction?

"We moved from Riverside, California," said Willow. She shifted the cat to her other arm and pushed her glasses up.

"Yeah?" I said, trying to seem bored. I didn't exactly want to hear her life story. For sure I didn't plan to tell her mine. Still, I'd never met anyone from

California. Why would someone from California move to Minnesota? Little did I know I was about to get the long version.

"My parents are artists, see," she said and took a big breath. "And sometimes they make a lot of money, and sometimes hardly any, and it's really expensive to live in California. We had this teeny little house, only three bedrooms and my dad used one for a studio, so that meant it was REAL crowded and we didn't even have a basement, because of earthquakes. All of us wanted to live in the country, there's so much pollution and crime and gangs and stuff in the city, but we couldn't afford it there, out in the country—well, mostly the country around there is desert anyhow—so when Mom found out about the artists' cooperative in Grand Marais, they checked it out and *voilà* here we are! We sold our little house and for the same money we got this big one and lots and lots of woods and five bedrooms and even a basement! And my dad'll have a studio, too, as soon as they can fix up that shed out back."

I was stunned. You have to understand that I'd been living with my dad for two and a half years. My dad hardly talks at all, and when he does, it's just a few words at a time. How could anyone talk this much? I must have looked dazed or something, because Willow leaned toward me and squinted.

"Are you okay?"

I nodded.

"What grade are you in?" she asked.

"Fifth," I said.

"I'm in fifth too!" Willow grinned. "Maybe we'll be in the same class!"

"I don't go to school."

"*What?*"

"Dad teaches me at home." I felt my ears burn as I spoke. I hoped she wouldn't notice the flaming color. I'd been doing correspondence courses since we moved. Dad said he didn't want me riding a school bus for two hours each day. It's true. It's a full hour one way. I didn't like home school at first, but after I got used to it, it was no big deal, not until Willow said "What?" like it was the craziest thing she'd ever heard.

"Oh, that's just *terrible!*" said Willow, then her hand flew to her mouth. "Oops, I mean, I wouldn't like it, but maybe you do. Rats. I was thinking we could ride the bus together. Did you used to take the bus? Don't you miss all the other kids?"

"Nope." I didn't know any other kids, not any that live around here. For some reason I was embarrassed to tell her that. Did she really wish we could ride the bus together? She didn't even know me!

At first when we moved here I thought about school every day. Then I found the cave and got used to not playing with other kids. I found things to keep me busy by myself, like learning birdcalls and drawing on the cave walls. Maybe I made myself get used to it because there wasn't a choice. Dad wanted me to learn at home and he isn't the kind of guy you disagree with. Telling Willow about home school felt weird.

"School starts on Monday," said Willow. "I'm totally nervous. Are Minnesota kids nice? You're nice, and you're from here. Do you think they'll know I'm from California?"

"You have an accent," I said, and her mouth dropped open. The cat jumped out of her arms and went over to sniff Rhonda. "It's not a heavy one, not like you were from Texas or anything."

Willow wiped pretend sweat off her forehead and said, "Whew!" Then she took a deep breath and kept talking. "I've never ridden a school bus before. Is that why you don't go to school? You don't want to ride the bus? We have to leave the house at a quarter to seven. Can you believe it? That's so *early*!"

"I like getting up early," I said. "That's when the birds and animals are around."

"Like bears and stuff? For *real*? Are they dangerous? Dad says there're a lot of bears here."

"I've seen a couple bears, but mostly I see small animals, rabbits and squirrels, lots of birds. There's a beaver family up at the lake. And once I saw a lynx."

"Is that like a mountain lion?"

"Not exactly." I'd never heard anyone ask so many questions at once. It was like Willow was dying of curiosity about a million things. I'd never met anyone like that before. I felt like I was being grilled.

"I bet you know tons of stuff about the woods, don't you?"

I shrugged.

"Have you lived here all your life? Would you take me to see the beavers?"

What a crazy way to talk! Willow kept asking me questions, two or three at a time. Which one was I supposed to answer? Did she really want to know all that stuff? Or did she just like to hear her own voice? When I ask my dad something, he answers. When he asks me something, I answer. It's not this jumble of questions all strung together. I took a deep breath.

"I'll take you to see the beavers if you want, and no, I only moved here a couple years ago."

"Where did you live before? Why did you move here?"

"St. Paul," I said, and then I stood up so fast I almost lost my balance. Suddenly I was sick of her zillion questions. What a snoop. I didn't want to talk about St. Paul, not to her, not to anyone. "I have to go now." I slapped my leg and Rhonda jumped up from where she was lying. "Let's go, Rhon." Willow stood up too. She had a puzzled look on her face. "See you around sometime," I said.

"I'm sorry I tried to hit you with that branch."

"It's okay." I turned around and headed for the opening. I could hear Willow behind me.

"Shouldn't you put out the fire?"

"You can do it," I said without turning around. "Just dump some dirt on it until it's not smoking." If she wanted to share the cave, she could do some of the work.

"Okay."

I was out the entrance in a second, and she was right behind me.

"How come you're in such a hurry?" Willow's voice sounded hurt.

"My dad's waiting for me," I lied. I was tired of sitting, tired of answering questions, tired of being cooped up with this blabbermouth. I wasn't used to all the noise. I still wished she'd been a boy. And I'm a private person, like my dad. Being around a snoopy girl made me nervous. Didn't her parents ever teach her to mind her own business? But there was something else that bugged me, something I hadn't thought about for a long time. My mom always talked like that, on and on barely taking a breath, especially when she and Grandma were together. I clenched my teeth and erased the thought of Mom and Grandma from my brain. I whistled for Rhonda, who had bounded through the brush after a chipmunk. The cold wind felt sharp on my face. Just then I heard a noise that froze me. A howl, far away.

"What was that?" whispered Willow. Rhonda whined. Her ears were sticking straight up, listening too, and then, there it was again! A long pitiful howl this time.

"Wolf," I said. We listened for a minute but didn't hear any more. I turned and looked at Willow.

Her thin arms were wrapped around herself. She looked terrified, and cold. "You should wear a coat," I told her, but she acted like she didn't hear me.

"Was it really a wolf?"

I nodded. Willow shivered.

I strained my ears to hear one more howl. I was sure it was King. Where was he? When would I get a glimpse of him? Then I remembered Willow shivering next to me and that whole pile of noisy sisters in the house below. Now I'd never see him, not with a whole bunch of new people in the area. They'd ruined everything by buying the Bennett House. *Everything*.

"Aren't you scared?" Willow asked.

"No," I said. She looked at me and frowned, but it wasn't a mad frown. Her eyes bored into me until I felt squirmy inside. I wanted to leave, but I didn't want to miss it if King howled one more time. Willow just kept staring.

"It's a sad sound, isn't it?" she said. "You never smile, do you, Perry Dubwah?"

Her words caught me off guard. I'd told her the right way to say my last name. Why did she always ask two questions like that! And so what if I don't smile much. Not everyone goes around grinning like a bucktoothed beaver all day long. She was such an invader! Coming up here and barging into my place like that. I slapped my leg and started for home. Rhonda hurried to catch up and heeled beside me perfectly. My cave was ruined. How could I have been stupid enough for one second to think I'd like being friends with that girl?

"Watch out for the wolf," Willow called after me. "And don't forget you said you'd show me where the beavers are, okay?"

I didn't answer her, and I didn't look back.

CHAPTER
6

I stayed away for a whole month. The leaves on all the trees turned yellow and bright red and orange. There were a couple big storms with a lot of rain and wind, and by the end of September, a lot of the trees were bare. More than once I found a thin layer of ice on Rhonda's water dish in the morning. It's not like I sat around watching the seasons change, though. I had plenty to keep myself busy.

My dad has a double business. As long as the weather is OK, he cuts wood and splits it to sell to people for firewood. When it starts to snow, he plows roads for the county and also for anyone who'll pay him. Winter was coming, and he had a lot of wood deliveries. Almost every day someone would call, and then I had to help stack the cords of wood on the big flatbed truck. He cuts wood on our property and has a permit to cut in certain parts of the national forest. When I was done with schoolwork, I helped with the wood. Dad and I always worked without talking much. That's our way. And when the wood was stacked, he would always drive off alone.

Sometimes Dad'll have a delivery way up into the Arrowhead, almost to Canada. Lots of times he delivers to people who live back in the woods, like we do. He'll take dirt roads that go for miles. He goes to some pretty out-of-the-way places. I bet a lot of kids would beg to go on those deliveries.

The first time Dad left me alone I was scared to death. I did beg to go with him, but he said someone had to stay behind in case the phone rang and another customer wanted wood. Now we have an answering machine, but I remember that first day like it was yesterday. "You stay here and hold down the fort," Dad said. "It'll make you more independent." I stopped begging and tried hard to be tough and independent, like my dad. I was just a little kid. I'd never been home by myself before. In St. Paul, Grandma had always stayed with me, or Aunt Stephie, or a babysitter. Now I was on my own.

Dad drove off with a truckload of wood and I stood on the porch, waving to him and smiling. I remember the smiling part really well because

I knew that if I kept smiling super hard my lower lip couldn't quiver. Soon the truck was out of sight, but I could still hear it. I kept smiling and waving until I couldn't hear the truck anymore and had to bite my lip hard to keep from being a wimp.

He wasn't gone long, really, but it sure felt like a long time to me. I learned an important lesson that day. I learned that it doesn't do any good to be scared or to beg. It doesn't change a thing. I turned on the radio, just to hear another voice. I threw a stick for Rhonda. The phone didn't ring. And my dad came back an hour later with an empty truck. I never asked to ride along again.

The month I stayed away from the cave I started my lessons with the fifth-grade assignments and papers that came with my correspondence stuff. A bunch of it was review. I'm a good reader, so Dad doesn't have to help me with school much. He gives me tests, but mostly I study on my own, so that's what I did. I spent about three hours a day with school stuff, the rest of the time I helped Dad or just hung around. I thought about my cave a lot.

Every Saturday we did what we always do, drove down to Grand Marais. Since I hardly ever go anywhere, this should have been the highlight of the week. In a way it was, because we also went to the library and grocery store, but there's one thing I hated about going to town. Picking up the mail. Maybe that doesn't sound like a big deal, but for me it was a huge deal ever since we moved. See, my mom will not stop writing to me.

Every week it was the same, and every week it made my stomach ache waiting for it to happen. It's like this. Dad would go into the post office, come out with a pile of mail in his hand, get back into the truck, sort through the mail, then hand me a letter. Some weeks there were two. He never said anything about my letters. Just looking at the fancy letters JK in the corner still bugs me sometimes. JK stands for Jennie Kuzak. That's who she is now. She started using that name about a six months ago. She wrote it on one of the envelopes. That's how I knew she must be married again. I didn't know if I should tell Dad. I didn't know if Dad got letters from her or not. He never said and I didn't want to ask. Mom was behind us, part of our past. She left. She didn't want us. We had a whole new life without her. I had taught myself not to want her. Her or her letters. The day I got the first Jennie Kuzak letter I got sick and puked for hours. Dad said it must have been something I ate.

After we went to the post office, we always went to the library. By the time I got around all those books, I'd be feeling better. My mom's letter was usually stuffed in my coat pocket, unread of course. Later, I'd add it to the pile in the grocery bag under my bed.

Right after we left St. Paul, my mom started writing. The first time I held one of her letters in my hand I had the weirdest feeling. Feelings of happiness clogged up my throat so I could hardly breathe. I missed my mom, even if she had left us, even if she hadn't said good-bye. I wished I were tiny enough to tear it open and climb inside. I wanted to read it, but I was only eight, and what if there were words I didn't know, or what if she wrote in cursive? I knew I'd have to ask Dad to read it to me, then; and I couldn't do that. He'd never offered either. And even if he had, maybe I'd have said no, because I wasn't just happy to get a letter from my mom, I was scared to death too. I was sure she was going to tell me why she'd left and I was pretty sure that part of the reason was me. One kid wasn't enough. When there were two kids, everything was fine. But when I was the leftover kid, she didn't want me. That's why I didn't open her letter. That first letter said Jennie Dubois on the front, up in the return address place.

I wasn't sure what to do with the first letter. I ended up putting it under my pillow, and that same night I had this nightmare. I dreamed I was in a dark, smothery hot place. My mom was small, like a kid or even a doll, and she was crying her head off and saying my sister's name. I ran to her and picked her up (she was still little in my dream), but she pushed me away and I fell down. I couldn't make her stop crying and she ran away.

I woke up shaking. I was as cold as an ice cube. I felt like I couldn't breathe. I knew I'd had that dream because of Mom's letter. It was the only explanation. So I knew I had to get rid of the letter before it gave me any more bad dreams. I tiptoed to the kitchen and found a match, even though I knew my dad would kill me if he found out. I took it back into my room and lit it and held that letter above the tiny flame. My hand shook. It was a bad letter. It made me have bad dreams. I was only eight back then, and that's what I thought. It was all Mom's fault I'd had that dream.

The flame lit up my whole room. It licked the

corner of the envelope. First the paper turned yellow, then the very tip started to turn black, then all of a sudden I smelled my mom's perfume coming up from that letter and I blew out the flame. I sniffed the letter. All I could smell was smoke, but now I couldn't burn it up. I can't explain why not, I just knew I couldn't do it. I couldn't burn up something that smelled like my mom. So I stuck it in a paper bag and hid it under my bed. That's where I've put her letters ever since. Once I started saving them, I kept doing it. I have a zillion letters, all unread. For a long time after I tried to destroy that first letter, I didn't have any more of those dreams.

After the post office, when Dad and I would go to the library, I'd stock up. You should see the stacks of books I've read. After Willow came, after I stopped going to my cave, I started reading everything I could about wolves. When I read all the books the Grand Marais library had, I ordered books from other libraries in the area. During the month of September, I read, I worked, I took Rhonda for walks, I listened for wolves. One of the books said scientists look for wolves by howling and when the wolves howl back, they know they're there. One windy Saturday I read a wolf book on the way back from Grand Marais. (It was a two-letter day.) When we got home I took Rhonda up to the lake and howled my head off. Pretty soon Rhonda was howling too. I howled and she howled and if I hadn't been trying so hard, it might have been sort of funny. My throat was sore for a couple days afterward. I never did hear a wolf.

Not a single day went by that month without me thinking about my cave. I missed it something awful. Of course, whenever I thought of it, I thought about Willow too. She's what kept me away. I was used to being by myself most of the time. I was used to silence and birds and forest animals. I told myself I was exactly like a lone wolf, like King. I didn't need people. But even though I tried not to, I thought about that skinny Willow girl every single day. I couldn't get her out of my head. Why did they have to come? I missed my hideout so much it felt like hunger.

Finally, on a gray drizzly day in early October, I gave in. I waited until I was positive everyone would be in school. There was no way she'd be around, no way I'd run into her. I'd just hike over to the cave and see how it was. Dad was out on a delivery. I put on a sweatshirt, made myself a lunch, and took off.

CHAPTER
7

By the time I got to the back side of the hill behind the cave, it was raining hard and I was soaked. The wind blew in gusts, and the leaves fell like giant brown snowflakes all around me. The ground was already thick with leaves. Rhonda went from one pile of leaves to another, sniffing underneath them for chipmunks and frogs. I hurried around the ledge. I couldn't wait to get inside. I was dying to see if Willow had demolished the whole place.

Rhonda bolted ahead and squeezed past me into the cave. I followed close behind her. It took a second for my eyes to get used to the dimness inside, but pretty soon I could see that nothing was out of place. Rhonda sniffed every single inch of the cave. The firewood hadn't been touched. My sitting stump was beside the fire ring as usual. The big rock was still where I'd dragged it. You'd never have known I'd been away for a whole month. I let out a huge sigh.

Maybe after she heard the wolf, Willow was too scared to come back. The big chicken. Maybe I could still come to my cave after all and have it to myself. If I came during school hours, no one would know. No one would see the smoke. That thought got me excited. I wouldn't be trespassing, since Willow said I could come here. I wondered if she'd told her parents about me, or about the cave. She'd said she wouldn't, but why should I trust her?

I shivered because I was so wet. No reason why I shouldn't have a fire right now, I thought. I pulled out my match case and went over to the woodpile. That's when I saw it. Right on top of the wood. A big brown spiral notebook. My heart sank. What was *that* piece of junk doing here?

I took down the notebook. My first thought was to add it to the wood and burn it up. That would show her. Leaving her stupid stuff in my cave. Willow had been here after all, and I was not exactly thrilled to find that out.

The outside of the notebook said SKETCHBOOK in big white letters. I opened it up. On the first page was a note, and it was pretty obvious who it was for.

READ THIS PERRY, it said. Willow's handwriting was huge and loopy. I kept reading.

At first I wasn't going to come back here but I changed my mind because it's so private. I hope you don't mind. I know it's on our property but it's your cave, really, because of the rule "Finders keepers losers weepers." I thought you were a pretty nice kid, even if you were so serious, so I decided to come here anyway and not mess anything up or make fires or anything. I like looking at your cave drawings. I also sit outside by the door and watch the birds. There're about a million of them around here. Sometimes I see animals too. Look inside for further details. Also look at the back of this book. I am giving you half of my allowance each month for rent. Don't get mad at me, OK? And please don't take this book. I keep it here so my baby brother won't scribble in it, but I don't care if you look at it.

Your tenant
(that's the person who pays you rent),
Willow

I flipped to the back of the book. Sure enough,

there was a white envelope taped to the back cover and inside were five one-dollar bills. *Rent?* I shook my head. What a dope. It really bugged me to find out she'd come back, even if she didn't mess anything up. On the other hand, it was pretty funny to think of her paying me rent, even though it was a screwy idea. I didn't want her money. What I wanted was my cave, all to myself, like I'd had it before. I sighed and stuffed the money in my jeans pocket. At least I could get a few Hershey bars. I read Willow's message again. *Look inside for further details,* it said. So I turned the page. I think what came out of my mouth was a cross between a gasp and *WOW!*

It was a raven, perfectly drawn in pencil. Actually, it was a bunch of ravens, or rather the same raven doing a bunch of things. Up in the left-hand corner, it was pecking at a stump. In the upper right-hand corner, it was fluffing its wings. In the middle drawing, it was strutting, the way ravens do when they find something cool and want to impress their friends. I looked closely. The raven had a couple tiny frog legs hanging from its beak. Down in the lower left corner, the raven sat on a branch with once head tucked under its wing. I turned the page.

A huge chickadee filled the next page. The drawing was so perfect I could practically feel the softness of the feathers on its breast. She'd even put delicate little claws on its feet and somehow made its eye twinkle. All with a stupid pencil! I turned the page. A chipmunk. Another page. A gray squirrel. Another page, three rabbits. Another page. A porcupine up in a tree.

It was amazing. My mouth hung open until it was practically dry. There were blue jays and woodpeckers and even a snake. And there weren't just animals either. There were all kinds of mushrooms, flowers, even a couple rocks. One page had six kinds of leaves. Each drawing was a surprise, not because I'd never seen any of that stuff, but because I'd never seen such great drawings; and by a *kid*! Willow had mentioned that her parents were artists. I guess it was a genetic thing that she was an artist too.

It took me a while to get through the book because I stared at every picture for a long time. I forgot all about being cold and wet. When I was almost to the end of the sketchbook, I turned to a page with a white-tailed buck. It reminded me of the dad deer in *Bambi*, all proud with its chest sticking out and a head full of antlers. I wondered where she'd seen it, probably right around here. These woods are full of deer. Suddenly I wondered if Willow knew about hunting season, about how dangerous it is to go out when the hunters are around. Someone should tell her, I thought. I turned to the next drawing and my heart stopped. I forgot all about hunters.

The picture was mostly of scenery. I recognized it right away. There's a little creek that flows past the Bennett House and beyond that there's a slope and then another ridge of granite, like the one my cave is part of. It's actually pretty far away, and because it's covered with trees, it's hard to see until late fall, when most of the leaves are gone. At one end of the ridge, there's a bare place about ten feet across, where nothing grows. I've sat up there once. It's just a big flat rock. You can see everything from there. I stared at Willow's drawing. On the bare gray rock, she'd drawn a wolf.

CHAPTER
8

My body went into automatic pilot. Sometimes you do something without thinking and it isn't until afterward that you know why you decided to do it. That's exactly what happened to me after I saw that wolf drawing. I tossed the sketchbook back on top of the woodpile, threw a couple scoops of dirt on the fire, hurried outside, and raced down the hill toward the Bennett House. I had to talk to Willow, even if she was a blabbermouthed girl. I had to know if she'd really, truly seen the wolf.

It was pouring, and the underbrush was soaked, and by the time I got to the front door I was dripping. Rhonda sat at my side, swishing her wet tail back and forth on the porch. I knocked really hard and heard footsteps, and before I could rehearse what I wanted to say, Willow's mom came to the door. I watched her through the glass.

She was at least as tall as my dad, and he's five-ten. Her long red hair was tied back in a ponytail and her wire-rimmed glasses had slid down her nose a ways. She had what looked like streaks of mud on her face. She pushed her glasses up with the back of a very dirty hand, wiped her hands on the grungy gray sweatshirt she was wearing, and pulled open the door. "Oh, hi!" she said with a huge smile. "I bet you're Perry! Willow hoped you'd come by." She looked down and saw Rhonda. "And there's the dog. Willow said it was a beauty and, really, it is."

I still hadn't said a word.

"You are Perry, right?" asked Mrs. Pestalozzi.

"Yeah," I said.

"Well, it's a good thing. How embarrassing if you weren't! Look at you! You're soaked. Come in, honey. Please don't stand out there another second."

"Oh, that's okay," I said. "I have to get home pretty soon." I felt my ears turn red. *Honey?* No one talks to me that way. Not anymore, that is. It made me feel squirmy. "I just wanted to leave Willow my phone number," I said. "Is that okay?"

Mrs. Pestalozzi opened the door up wide. "Of course, but you can't stand out there in the rain like that, come in. I'll grab paper and a pencil."

I told Rhonda to stay and stepped inside. Mrs. Pestalozzi smiled again, then she headed off into another part of the house. The house smelled like chicken soup, the homemade kind. I swallowed. I'd forgotten to eat my lunch and I was starving. "Come into the kitchen, Perry," she called, so I wiped my feet and followed her down the hall and through the dining room.

The kitchen was the biggest disaster area I have ever seen. I think it might have qualified as a bio-hazard. I'm not kidding. There were a million dishes on the counters and in the sink, and there were toys on the floor and a little jacket and at least five shoes of different sizes. In the place by the window where normally a table and chairs would be, there was a potter's wheel. I'd seen a picture of one in a book, so I knew what it was. There was a bucket of clay on the floor beside it, several wet-looking pot things on a board stretched between two concrete bricks, and a stool. And there was a little kid in a highchair, eating Cheerios off the tray.

Mrs. Pestalozzi rummaged in a drawer. "I can't find a pencil anywhere," she said. "Bill?" she yelled at the top of her voice. "BILL!" A man answered from what had to be the basement. Mrs. Pestalozzi opened a door at the other end of the kitchen and yelled down, "Toss me a pencil, would you, dear?" A second passed, then a pencil came flying past Mrs. Pestalozzi's head and landed in the mess of pots and pans behind her. "Thanks!" she yelled downstairs and slammed the door shut. She turned to me. "Did you see where it landed?" I pulled the pencil out from between a frying pan full of old egg crust and a pot that looked like it had had spaghetti in it for about a year and handed it to her.

"Thanks," she said. "Sorry about the mess. I've got a show coming up and I have to finish fifty mugs before I go. The only time I can work is when the kids are at school. It's a pottery show. That's why my hands are dirty like this."

I nodded.

She sounded just like Willow, the way she went on and on. The baby pounded his highchair tray. Cheerios flew all over the place. Mrs. Pestalozzi rummaged through the same drawer. "I know I've got to have a piece of paper somewhere," she said, and when she didn't find one, she pulled a can of Chef Boyardee spaghetti from the shelf, tore off the label, flipped the label over, and held it up against the wall to write. "Okay, Perry. Your phone number."

"BOY!" yelled the baby.

"Ian, hush," said Mrs. Pestalozzi.

"BOY!" Little Ian pointed at me. "BOY."

"My number is 255-2901," I said. Just then a smell hit my nostrils. It was coming from Ian, and it wasn't chicken soup. Mrs. Pestalozzi must have smelled it too.

"Oh, Ian, did you poop? Is that 255-2901?"

"Yeah," I said.

"BOY!" said Ian.

"His name is *Perry*," said Mrs. Pestalozzi.

"Poopy," said Ian.

"Do you live very far from here?"

"No," I said, "not if you know the trails. It takes me only ten minutes." Even though Mrs. Pestalozzi was being friendly, I felt kind of like I was smothering in that house. There was so much junk! And the smells, and the baby, everything made me itch. I wanted to ask if they knew about the wolf. When did Willow see it? Did she see it more than once? "Just give my number to Willow, and if she wants, tell her to call me. I have a couple of important questions for her."

"Will do," said Mrs. Pestalozzi. "She'll be happy you came by. She's been kind of lonely lately. Maybe next time you can stay longer."

"Yeah, maybe," I said. "Well, I gotta go now." The poop smell was really strong. I hadn't smelled that smell for a long time. I hadn't been around any babies for years. I looked at Ian one more time. His cheeks were bright red and almost perfectly round, and he had sky blue eyes. His hair was dark and curly and there were Cheerio crumbs in it. He smiled and pointed at me with a fat little finger.

"Berry?" he said.

Berry. I'd forgotten all about that name. I'd stuffed it away with a bunch of other things I didn't think about anymore. I felt my throat go tight, and I swallowed. I pulled the dollar bills out of my pocket and stuffed them in Mrs. Pestalozzi's hand. "Give these back to Willow, okay?" I said, and without saying another word, I hurried down the hall and let myself out.

I had so many thoughts swimming around in my head that the walk home seemed to take only a few seconds, even in the pouring rain. Willow was using my cave, but she wasn't messing it up. She'd seen a wolf, or *maybe* she'd seen it, and I had to find out which. Her mom was nice; their house was a pit. The thing I kept thinking about, though, was Ian, how being around that baby, even for a couple of minutes, had brought back a lot of memories. That's why I'd felt like choking. I'd thought I was all done with those kinds of feelings, the bad ones that make a guy act like a wuss.

Dad was home when I got there, but aside from telling me that it's stupid to go out in bad weather without rain gear, he didn't ask where I'd been or what I'd done. He said he had a delivery and asked me to stick around. I felt like telling him about the Pestalozzi house, about Willow's mom. I wanted to tell him about Ian, but then that choking feeling came back and I didn't say a word. Dad didn't want to hear about it. If he did, he would have asked me. I wanted to talk to him about the wolf, but I didn't. *Had Willow seen it?* I was dying to know. I could hardly stand thinking about it. Would she call? And what if she did? It's not like I wanted to be *friends*. I wanted information. That's it.

I changed into dry clothes and gulped down two sandwiches and a glass of milk as Dad's truck rumbled away from the house down the dirt road. Then I grabbed my latest wolf book, went into my room, and flopped down on my bed to read and wait for the phone to ring.

CHAPTER
9

It rained so hard it sounded like someone was dumping marbles on the roof. Pretty soon I dozed off. I dreamed I heard a wolf howling and went looking for it in my closet. (Dreams are weird that way.) As soon as I opened the closet door, the sound turned into a baby crying and I was scared; but now I was stuck in the closet and it was totally dark. I started yelling but no sound came out of my mouth, and all I could hear was the baby crying and me sort of squeaking, trying to yell, and then I jerked myself awake because the phone was ringing. I jumped up and ran out to the kitchen.

"Hello?"

"It's me, Perry," said Willow's voice. "Mom said you came by. How are you?"

"Fine," I said, hoping you can't hear another person's heart beating over the telephone. "Did you really see all the stuff in that drawing book?"

"You mean all the animals?"

"Yeah."

"I saw all of them except the deer. I copied him off a calendar. I love drawing animals."

"So you saw the wolf!"

"Yeah, and it was so scary. I'm glad it was far away. I get the shivers just thinking about it."

"But WHEN?" I asked. "WHEN did you see it?"

"It was yesterday."

Yesterday! I felt totally ripped off. Why should she be the lucky one? I'd heard the wolf first. I'd even given it a name. It was unfair that Willow should see it. "What did it do?" I asked her. "Are you sure it wasn't some dog?"

"It stood there for a long time, then it howled once. That's how I knew it wasn't a dog. It was that same sound we heard. Remember? It was horrible, so sad sounding. Then I swear I only blinked, and it was gone. I drew the picture from memory."

"You are so stinking lucky," I said. "I'd give *any-thing* to have seen it."

"Wouldn't you be scared?"

"I wouldn't be scared at all."

"Liar."

"I'm serious," I said. "Wolves hate being around people, so it's hard to get a look at them."

"I bet it would try to eat me," said Willow.

"No way," I said. "No one has ever been attacked by a healthy wolf, I read it in a book. Lots of people think wolves are dangerous, but they aren't—except to dogs and other pets, sheep, stuff like that." It was kind of amazing to hear myself say so many words at one time. Maybe being around those Pestalozzis was rubbing off on me.

"Dogs?" asked Willow.

"Yeah, keep those little dogs of yours in at night."

"*What?*" Willow yelled in my ear.

"The cat too," I said. I didn't mean to shock her, but it's true. You have to keep track of your pets in wolf country.

After that Willow had a million questions about wolves. Good thing I'd read all those books. I could tell she was impressed because she kept saying, "Wow, you know everything." Well, not everything, but it felt pretty good for her to think that.

I asked Willow a few questions about the wolf: the color, how big did it look, could she tell if it was a male or a female, stuff like that. She said it was real dark gray, almost black, and shaggy. She couldn't tell the sex.

"Do you think it'll come back, Perry?" she asked.

"I hope so. I want to see it." Boy, did I ever want to see it.

"We could put out bait," said Willow. "Maybe a piece of bacon."

"No way!" I said. "That's a crazy idea. Don't you know the rule? Never *ever* feed wild animals?"

"Oh, yeah," said Willow. "I forgot about that. So they won't get dependent on humans."

"Yeah, and so they won't associate human scent with food. Otherwise, they might stop being scared of people."

"I definitely want the wolves to stay scared of me," said Willow.

"Me too," I said. I wanted to tell her no sane wolf would come within a mile of a girl who talks as much as she does, but I kept my mouth shut.

Willow asked why the wolf was by itself. "I thought they hung around in herds."

"*Packs*," I said, and then I told her how sometimes a wolf will go off on its own, away from its family pack, to look for a mate, when I heard Dad pull into the yard. All of a sudden I realized it was dark out. I'd been blabbing without even thinking.

"I gotta go," I said. We'd talked for an hour. I

couldn't believe it. I felt stupid, talking to a girl like that. It was her fault, though. For asking so many questions.

"Perry," said Willow, "why don't we go looking for that wolf?" Now it was my turn to be suprised.

"Together?"

"Yeah, let's go look for it, track it in the woods. I bet you know how. You said they aren't dangerous, right?"

"I don't think so—"

"Then if we even get a peek we'll be lucky, but at least maybe we could find footprints or wolf poop. It would be so fun. It would be like an outdoor adventure. Do you like nature programs on TV? It would be like being in a nature program. Do you like *National Geographic* specials? I could bring my camera. I got a camera for my last birthday. It has a zoom lens."

"I thought you were scared," I said. Hiking around with a girl was not my idea of a good time. I heard Dad shut off the truck motor.

"If I went with a wolf expert like you, I wouldn't be scared."

I felt my lips curl into a tiny smile. A wolf expert. Hah.

"And now my mom has met you," said Willow, "and she said, 'He's a very sweet boy,' so I know she wouldn't mind me just looking around, as long as we kept our distance from anything, you know, dangerous."

"We probably wouldn't see a thing," I said. I'd already decided I wanted to go look for King. Maybe taking another person wouldn't be so bad. "You'd have to be super quiet." I said. "As in no blabbing." I heard the truck door slam shut. I didn't want Dad to catch me on the phone. I didn't want to explain about talking to a girl, but still, I couldn't exactly hang up without saying good-bye. Dad always sweeps out the truck bed after a delivery. I had time, but not much.

"I'll be as quiet as a mouse," said Willow.

"Oh, right," I said.

"I will. And maybe we'll see other animals. Maybe when I grow up I'll be a famous nature photographer and it'll be all because of you, Perry Dubwah, outdoor boy of the woods. Please?"

"Oh, all right," I said. "But we have to do it before hunting season starts."

"Wolf hunting? They hunt wolves?"

"No, *deer* season," I said. "Wolves are protected."

"You mean people go out and shoot the poor deer?"

"Yeah. They eat them too. Actually, bow hunting started a couple weeks ago."

"As in bow and arrow hunting?"

"Right. But there aren't that many bow hunters. We haven't seen any since we moved here. It's open season you have to worry about. It starts the first weekend in November and lasts two weeks. Some of those guys shoot at anything that moves."

"We better look for the wolf right away, then," said Willow. "How about Saturday, around nine. I'll meet you at the cave, okay?"

"Earlier is better," I said. "How about seven?"

"Seven? You're nuts!"

"Yes or no?" I asked. "That's when animals are out the most." I had to get off the phone.

"All right!" said Willow. "See you Saturday then."

"Okay, bye." I pushed the hang-up button on the phone. The doorknob turned and Dad pulled open the door.

"Any customers call while I was out?" he asked, glancing at the phone in my hand.

"Nope," I said and put the phone back in its cradle.

CHAPTER
10

I didn't really expect we'd find King. From my reading I knew that wolves have fairly large territories, sometimes covering several square miles. I also knew that they avoid people at all costs, and they can smell us a long way off. Still, I couldn't wait to try. Even if we found a footprint it would be cool.

We. That was the funny part, just thinking about hiking around with someone else, a person, I mean. Before, it was just me and Rhonda. Now I had someone else to explore with and it gave me an exciting feeling whenever I thought about it. It also made me nervous. Willow had seemed so irritating at first. Would we have fun? Would it be weird, being with a girl? It's not like anyone was going to see us. A couple times I wanted to call her and tell her to forget it, but I didn't have her

number and I didn't want to call information.
I counted down the days until Saturday.

Friday night I told Dad I'd be getting up early
the next morning. He just nodded. I get up early
lots of times. It's not exactly news. We were eating
dinner, meat loaf and baked potatoes. I know how
to cook a bunch of things. Me and Dad take turns.
I like to make spaghetti, macaroni and cheese,
hamburgers. Meat loaf is my speciality. I like squish-
ing up the meat and raw eggs and bread with
my hands. Mom used to let me mix it that way
when I was little. Anyway, Dad was peeling the alu-
minum foil off of his potato when he asked about
my schoolwork.

"How's that math coming?" He folded the foil up
and put it beside his plate.

"Okay," I said. I broke open my potato and put a
slab of butter into it.

"Are you having any trouble with it?"

"No." Math is my easiest subject. Dad knew that.
About once a week he'd say, "How's that math coming?" and my answer was always the same. It never
bothered me before that he asked me the same
thing over and over again, but that night it did. For
once, why couldn't he ask me about something else,

something besides schoolwork. I hadn't thought about his questions before. After the accident, Dad got real quiet. It's hard to explain. It's not like he was a big talker before, it's just that afterward, he talked even less. I remember Mom crying and yelling at him for not talking to her. I remember thinking it was a stupid thing to be mad about. I mean, if a person didn't want to talk, why should he have to? It's a free country, right?

Dad and I had lived for almost three years without talking much. Dad didn't like to talk. And when other people talked too much, like my mom, after Livvy died, Dad would get up and leave the room. I learned right away not to blab at my dad. I knew if I did, he'd find something to do someplace else. If I wanted him around, I had to keep quiet. That's why what I said next totally surprised me.

"I'm going looking for a wolf tomorrow," I said. "I've heard one howling a couple times." I stirred the melted butter into the potato. I peeked up across the table at Dad. His black eyebrows shot up. This may sound weird to people who talk about stuff every single day, but in all the time we'd lived up here, I'd never told Dad what I did when I played. He'd never asked.

"Oh, yeah? You sure?"

"Yeah. Remember those new people I told you about?"

Dad nodded.

"Well, one of the girls, Willow, saw a wolf up on that big granite slab. She drew a picture of it. She has a big family and her mom's an artist. I think her dad is too. We're going to go looking for footprints, stuff like that."

I wanted to look into his eyes, figure out what he was thinking, read his mind, but I stabbed a piece of meat loaf and dipped it in ketchup instead. Would he act nervous and get up and go into another room or outside? Would he ask me more questions? I washed the bite of meat loaf down with a gulp of milk. For some reason it didn't taste as good as it usually does. I sneaked a look at my dad. He was staring at me. At first, that's what I thought. Then I looked again, and I realized he was staring past me or through me, or I don't really know how to explain it except that it wasn't *me* he was looking at. I wished he'd stop.

"I thought you didn't like girls," Dad said.

I shook my head hard, automatically. "I don't," I said. "It's just that there's no one else—" I swallowed. I picked a piece of foil off my potato and didn't finish what I had started to say. *There's no one else to do stuff with.* I could tell Dad was still looking at me. I concentrated on my potato.

"You be careful tomorrow," said Dad.

"Okay," I said. "Do you like the meat loaf?"

"You bet," said Dad. He picked up his fork and knife and started cutting.

My stomach had tied itself into a big knot. The bright red ketchup, the brown meat, the white-and-yellow potato, they all looked gross now. For a minute I just sat there. My heart was racing. Up until now I'd kept myself hidden from him, kept all my thoughts rolled up like a sleeping bag, just like he did with me. We're real quiet guys, me and Dad. That's why I didn't tell him all about my cave, or learning the birdcalls, or about hearing King howl. And now all of a sudden, I was telling him about Willow, practically blabbing.

Did he think I *liked* her?

I took another gulp of milk. It's not like I was lonely or anything. I didn't want Dad to think that. I was tough, as tough as he was, and I liked living alone in the woods, just like he did. We had our privacy. That's one good thing about keeping your mouth shut. No one ever knows what's happening on the inside. That's maximum privacy for sure. That's what Dad and I wanted most, wasn't it?

I was still thinking about it as I lay awake in bed that night. The wind wailed across the chimney and rattled the windowpanes. Before, whenever the wind blew like that, I'd felt perfectly cozy. In my own bed I was safe from the night, the bitter north winds that blow down from Canada. But for some reason I couldn't get warm. I got up and dug another blanket out of my closet and snuggled down into my covers. I curled into a little ball and hugged my knees. Outside the wind moaned, low and harsh. I didn't want to hear it. That sound was making me cold. I put my head under my pillow.

I was almost asleep when I heard something that got my attention. It sounded like a wolf howling. I listened for a few moments and didn't hear it again. Probably just the wind, I told myself and drifted off to sleep. That night I dreamed I saw my dad running through the woods. He looked scared, like something was chasing him. I tried to run after him but my legs would only go in slow motion. I yelled his name over and over again, but he kept running away. And then, just like that, he turned into a wolf and disappeared between the trees. I jerked awake and lay staring at the moonlight stripes on my wall. The wind howled again. I knew it must be the wind. I put my head under my pillow so I wouldn't hear it. After a while I fell asleep again, and if I dreamed anything after that, I don't remember.

CHAPTER
11

Dad was gone on a delivery when I woke up the next morning. I ate a bowl of cereal and left for the cave without Rhonda. She didn't like being left behind and I could hear her whining through the door. I got to the cave at seven on the dot. It wasn't dark, but it wasn't light either. Halfway in between, I'd say. The windstorm had blown the leaves off everything but the evergreen trees. A big pile of leaves had collected at the entrance to the cave. I stepped over them and went inside. I pulled a banana out of my pocket and peeled it. For a minute I wished I'd brought Rhonda. What if Willow didn't show up?

I wasn't used to sharing my cave, or any of the woods around it. It wouldn't be any big deal if Willow didn't show up. I kept telling myself that while I ate my banana.

I'd probably been there only a couple minutes when I heard a voice. "You in there, Perry?" It was Willow. I stuffed the end of the banana into my mouth and wiped my hands on my jeans.

She poked her head into the cave. "Hi." She tried to squeeze in the entrance, but she had on a backpack and wouldn't fit. "Oh, shoot, " she said. "I'm too fat with this backpack."

"Just hang on," I said. "I'll come out."

"I think I'm stuck," said Willow. "Would you mind pushing me?" I pushed and she squirmed, and finally she popped out. "Whew!" she said, brushing off the front of her jacket. "Just think what would have happened if you weren't here to rescue me!" She grinned that crooked grin and pushed her glasses up into place with a gloved finger. "Don't just stand there! Let's go find the wolf!" Willow whirled around and took off toward the big rock. I caught up and walked beside her. A bunch of stuff was going on in my head.

First of all, I was having a hard time not thinking of those woods as *my* woods. They were really Willow's woods, or her parents', now that they owned the land, but I'd been the only person around for a long time. I'd hiked all these trails with Rhonda. I knew the shortcuts. I knew where the trails got swampy in the summer. I knew where the blueberries grew in the open spaces. Now here I was, walking with a girl. Not that it mattered *that* much that she was a girl. I mean, even if she'd been a guy, it still would have felt like I was sharing something maybe I wasn't ready to share. I didn't talk to her. I wasn't trying to be mean or anything, I just didn't know what to say.

Of course, Willow talked and talked. She told me about school, about her favorite subjects (art and science), the snotty girls in her class (Evie, Maureen, and Casey), and the worst school lunch she'd ever eaten (wiener winks). She said she'd read a book on wolves. She said she wasn't scared anymore. She said she called the International Wolf Center in Ely and that her dad said they could go visit it sometime. That made me jealous. I'd always wanted to go there, but I didn't want to ask Dad. It's pretty far away. Willow then told me how she wanted to take a picture of a wolf and have her dad make a painting. "He loves wildlife," she said.

She took a break from talking, to take a breath, I think, and in that second I thought of something to ask her. "How come you're all bundled up like that?" Willow was wearing what looked like a brand-new jacket. It was definitely a winter jacket—probably down, because it was so puffy that it made her look like a brightly colored marshmallow. It was green and purple and had a hood with fur around the edge. The hood was pulled up and tied in place. It made her face look really small.

"It's *freezing* out here," said Willow.

"It's in the forties," I said. "It isn't cold. You don't know what cold is." She didn't, either. Not if she was from California.

"The kids at school said it goes down to twenty below," said Willow. She had to turn her body sort of sideways to see me. Her hood was really cinched tight.

"It gets lower than that all the time. And if you add the windchill—"

"What's windchill?" asked Willow. "The kids talk about it."

"That's when the wind blows AND it's really cold. So, say it's twenty below and the wind is blowing, it feels more like thirty below, get it? Your skin freezes a lot faster." It felt good to know a bunch of stuff that she didn't.

"Freeze your *skin*?" Willow turned and stared popeyed at me. "That's *gross!* "

"It's dangerous," I said. "I have really warm gear and good boots, but I stick close to home when it's that cold."

"Do you still go to the cave? Doesn't the fire keep you warm?"

"No, the heat goes right out. A campfire isn't very efficient for heating."

"Rats," said Willow. She was quiet for a minute. "I like going to the cave."

"Me too," I said. I hated those cold days when I couldn't go to the cave. One year we had three weeks straight of twenty below temps. I thought I'd go stir-crazy.

Willow and I walked down along the creek until we came to a place where it was narrow enough to jump across. Then we started up the back of the big hill, where Willow had seen the wolf.

"Stop, stop," said Willow about a fourth the way up. She was huffing and puffing really hard. "I have to rest." She sat on a log and took off her backpack. Then she loosened her hood and let it fall back. "Whew. I'm burning up." She looked at me and smiled. Then she took off her gloves and stuffed them into her pocket. She unzipped her jacket. "Aren't you going to ask what I have in my backpack?"

I have to admit I'd been curious. Her backpack was stuffed full and I could tell it was heavy. "Okay. What?"

Willow unzipped the top and reached in. "First of all, tah-DAH! Snacks!" She pulled out a one-pound bag of M&M's and handed it to me. Then she pulled out a bag of Oreo cookies and handed that to me too. And a box of vanilla wafers. And a Thermos. And a bag of Cheetos, which had gotten kind of squished. Two cans of soda pop, one Coke, one Sprite. She put those on the ground. I couldn't hold anything else. "I hope you're hungry," she said.

"Is this what you eat for breakfast every day?" I asked.

"No, silly. This is hiking food." She pulled out a camera. It was a Minolta with a big lens. She hung it around her neck. Then she pulled out a small sketchpad and a pencil case. Last she pulled out a full roll of toilet paper. "In case I have to go," she said, and then she giggled.

I stood there with my arms full of junk food. The bag of cookies was open. The smell made my mouth water. "Come on, sit down, Perry Dubwah," said Willow. "Don't just stand there." She unzipped the empty backpack all the way open and laid it out on the ground. "Put the food down on that," she said. The ground was still damp from the rain the day before. I guess she didn't care that her backpack might get muddy. I sat down beside her.

"You sure don't talk much," said Willow. She handed me the Oreos and tore open the M&M's. "Do you like Oreos? Want some hot chocolate?" I nodded. She twisted the top off the Thermos and filled the cup. "I guess we'll have to share. I won't backwash." She took a sip, then handed me the cup. "Do you like to eat the white junk in the middle of the cookie first, or do you eat the whole thing at once?" I stared at the Oreo in my other hand. I'd never thought about it before. I guess she didn't really expect an answer, because she kept right on talking.

"My dad's real quiet like you, too," she said. "But he smiles all the time." I didn't have much time to think about her comment because a couple seconds later she grabbed my arm. Hot chocolate spilled on my leg.

"Jeez!" I said. "Watch it."

"Oh, look!" said Willow. "Look, over there! I need my camera. *My camera!*"

CHAPTER
12

It was only a rabbit, about fifty yards away and walking in that careful lippity loppity way they do. It was brown, the same color as the fallen leaves, but when I looked carefully I could see it was starting to turn white for the winter. If it hadn't been moving, we would never have seen it. Willow aimed her camera at the rabbit and fiddled with the lens. *Click.* "Got it," she said in a whisper. "My dad gave me his old camera for my birthday. Isn't it cool?"

"Yeah." It was cool. I have a little instamatic camera. The pictures always turn out lousy.

"What's your dad like? Does he like photography?" asked Willow. She opened the box of vanilla wafers and took out a huge handful. She stuffed them in her mouth and looked at me, waiting for me to answer.

"My dad doesn't have any hobbies," I said. "He cuts wood."

"Does he wear red plaid shirts? Is he a lumberjack?"

"No. We own about 320 acres of woods. He cuts wood and sells it. For firewood. It's a private business." I popped a cookie in my mouth.

"Did your mom die?"

Her question was so unexpected that for a second I sat there with my mouth open. A couple cookie crumbs fell out onto my jacket and I snapped my mouth shut. I must have looked like an idiot. I was in shock, that's all.

"No, she didn't *die*," I said finally. I brushed the crumbs off my front and stood up. I handed Willow the hot-chocolate cup. "Are we going to look for the wolf, or what?"

"Okay, okay." said Willow. "So, are your parents divorced? My aunt and uncle got a divorce. Where does your mom live? Do you go for visits? My cousins go every weekend." Willow chomped down a couple more cookies and started packing the backpack.

One of the hardest things in the world is when someone asks you questions you don't even want to think about. Why did Willow have to be such a snoop? I stared at my feet. Part of me wanted to leave right then and there, forget all about this big-mouth girl and her millions of questions. I had never talked out loud about my mom leaving us, not to anyone. My parents were divorced. It happens to a lot of kids. It's just that I'd never talked about that either. I wanted to walk away. But I couldn't do it.

I'd been alone for so long that I'd forgotten how *fun* it is to be with someone else, even if that someone barges into your life without being asked. I'd forgotten how much fun I'd had playing with the other boys in my neighborhood in St. Paul, riding up and down the alley on our bikes, playing with Tonka trucks in the sandbox. Catching bees in a jar. Those were good times. I'd made myself not think about them so I wouldn't be lonely. But now I was used to being alone, right? I didn't need friends. But I couldn't make myself get up and leave.

Willow put the cookies and two cans of pop back into the backpack, and as she worked, she hummed a little song. I knew the song too, I just couldn't think of the name. "What's that song?" I asked. I stooped over and picked up the Cheetos to help.

"It's from *Sesame Street*. You know, the one that

goes *Who are the people in your neighborhood?*" She took the Cheetos from me and stuffed them into the backpack. "Katie, that's my littlest sister, and Ian, that's the baby you saw, they love that show. Katie's in first grade and she still watches it. Can you believe it? *A first grader!* They got up at six and were watching it this morning. Some days I can't get the stupid songs out of my head."

Sesame Street. I hadn't thought of that show for a long time. I watched it every day when I was little. Bert and Ernie were my favorites. Livvy always liked Big Bird best. It's one of the first words she said. BeeBo. How could I forget that? She'd called Big Bird BeeBo. I'd forgotten about BeeBo. In fact, I'd forgotten the whole thing until right that second. I felt my face get cold. My ears rang, and in my mind I saw my grandma putting a bright yellow stuffed Big Bird doll into a little white casket.

"Are you okay?" asked Willow. She was looking at me kind of funny. I nodded and the awful memory disappeared. "Ready to go?" she asked. I turned my back on her and started up the hill without answering. My mouth felt dry. Something was going wrong. Things I didn't want to think about, things I'd kept locked up for a long time, kept popping into my head. It had to be Willow's fault. Willow and all her questions. I walked fast.

She didn't say anything for about a hundred yards. I could hear her behind me, following me, breathing hard. I could hear my heart pumping in my head. Think about finding the wolf, I told myself.

"Perry," said Willow, interrupting my thoughts.

"What?" No more questions. I wanted to yell it in her face.

"I won't ask about your mom anymore."

"Good," I said, and hiked to the top of the hill full speed.

We didn't find a single wolf footprint. I'm not surprised either, not with all the rain we'd had the day before. I suggested we split up and look around in the bushes, try to find some kind of evidence, a pile of wolf droppings, maybe some fur or even bones or parts of something the wolf might have eaten. That's another way scientists know wolves are around. They find dead deer and moose or parts of rabbits, stuff like that. Anyway, we didn't find anything. The sun came out and made everything look warm and golden and I didn't feel so mad at Willow for being nosy. Maybe she can't help it, I thought. Maybe her nosiness is like a mental defect or something.

We stood on the flat rock and looked out over the country. Willow tied her jacket around her waist and took a picture of her house from the rock. "You can see for ever from up here," she said, and I had to agree. The woods stretched on for miles. After she took the picture, Willow suggested we put out some Cheetos to try to attract the wolf, but I gave her a dirty look and that ended that. Finally we sat on the rock and worked on the snacks.

I was starving and thirsty. I bet I ate half that bag of M&M's. When we got to the cans of pop, Willow suggested we shake them and have a contest, see which makes more foam, Coke or Sprite. I took the Sprite. We shook the cans hard.

"Okay," said Willow, "we have to pop them open at exactly the same time. Ready? One, two, three." *POP!* White foam sprayed up into the air from my green can. Willow held her can and wiggled it around. "Look! Fireworks!" One of her hands slipped and the spray hit me in the face. "Oops," she said.

"HEY!" I yelled.

"Sorry, sorry!" said Willow, then she grinned

wickedly and pointed her can at me. I jumped back, but not before getting a big stream of Coke fizz right in the face. I aimed my can of pop at her, but missed her head because she ducked to one side. Willow slurped some pop from the top of her can. "Mmm. I'm thirsty," she said. "I wonder if there's any Coke left in this can." Coke was dripping from my nose and one of my ears. My hair was wet. I could feel a little Coke stream dripping down my neck. I wiped my face and tried to look mad.

Instead, I started to laugh.

Willow laughed too. She doubled over and hooted, and then she snorted. The snorting really got to me. I laughed until I could hardly get my breath and Willow kept laughing and snorting. She sounded just like a pig. Just when I'd think I was done laughing, she'd snort again and it's like I couldn't control myself. All because of a stupid soda pop contest.

"You should have seen the look on your face, Perry Dubwah," she said. "This is what you looked like." She opened her mouth in fake surprise and crossed her eyes. Looking at her imitating me made me crack up again.

It's stupid, really, if you think about it. Two kids spray each other with pop and then have a laugh attack. It was fun, though. When we were done laughing we ate a bunch more cookies.

Finally it was time to go. I'd promised Dad I'd be back by ten so we could go to town. I had a big stack of books to take back to the library that day. We packed our trash into Willow's backpack and I offered to carry it.

"Oh, *right*," she said with her hands on her hips. "I carry it full all the way up this big hill, and then you offer to carry it when it doesn't weigh a thing. Nice guy."

"Next time I'll carry it full," I said.

"Promise?" asked Willow.

"Yeah, sure."

"How about tomorrow? Can we go looking for the wolf again?"

"Okay."

"Deal," said Willow. She stuck out her right hand and we shook.

"Deal," I said. I let go of her warm, sticky hand and headed down the hill. Willow hummed *Who are the people in your neighborhood?* all the way to her house. For some reason, it didn't bug me anymore.

CHAPTER
13

Dad and I drove to town after I got back from hiking with Willow. That Saturday was a one-letter day. Yellow envelope. Size and feel of a small card. When I first started getting letters, it upset me a lot. I wanted to read them, and at the same time, I didn't. After a while of not reading them, I got used to it and didn't want to anymore. But that particular day, there was a part of me that really wanted to open that yellow envelope. I could feel it in my back pocket all the way home. *She left us forever,* I told myself over and over again. *I don't want to read her stupid letters.*

When we got home, Dad and I chopped a bunch of wood. Dad used the diesel log splitter, but I chopped by hand until my arms about fell off. I thought about looking for the wolf while I chopped. It helped some.

Willow had said she couldn't meet me until after Mass on Sunday. They drove in to St. John's Church in Grand Marais every week and didn't get back until one o'clock. We met at the cave at two. "I bet we'll see something today!" she yelled as she came up the hill. Her crooked smile spread from ear to ear and her cheeks were red. Sweat made her hair stick to her forehead. I noticed she didn't have the winter coat on this time. I offered to carry the heavy backpack and we took off for the lake at the edge of our property.

The day was sunny and almost warm. I say almost because as long as we were walking I felt warm, but as soon as we stopped and my sweat had a chance to dry, the cold seeped into my clothes. It was the time of year when you can never get your clothes right, either you wear too many or not enough. The sunshine had that thin, clear autumn feel, and the bare trees made the country-side look empty. We hiked between the trees in the general direction of my house, and with each step the rotting leaves and mud sent their smells up to our noses. Winter was definitely on the way.

Of course, Willow wanted to see where I lived. We got pretty close to the house, crossing and then following along the dirt road to the place where you turn into the long driveway. I wasn't going to take her there, but then she said she had to go to the bathroom and what could I say? I still think it was a lie. Anyway, I took her to my house. Dad wasn't around. I showed her the inside: the living room, the kitchen, my room. "I love all your wolf posters," she said.

"I got them at Kmart in Duluth," I said. "That one has glow-in-the-dark eyes." It was my favorite. It was fun to show someone my room. I was thinking it's a good thing I didn't leave any Jockey shorts lying around, when Willow sniffed and made a face.

"Your room smells like gym socks," she said, and then she whirled around and went into the hall. "Where's the bathroom?"

I pointed at the door. I wasn't sure whether or not I'd just been insulted. Did I stink or something? Willow popped into the bathroom. I sniffed my pits. Nothing. Just then she stuck her head out the door.

"I thought maybe you lived in a log cabin or something," she said, sort of sounding disappointed. "This is just a regular house."

I was starting to wish I hadn't brought her here. I had that same feeling as when she'd found my cave, and it was a feeling of invasion. Nobody but Dad had ever been in our house since we'd moved—not past the living room, anyway. No one had been in my room, seen my posters, sniffed the air. I heard the toilet flush, then the water in the sink, then the door opened. "You'd better go before we leave," she said. I ignored her. Like I need someone to tell me when to take a leak!

"Do you want to go up to the lake, or not?" I asked.

"Oh, goodie! I love lakes!" Willow said. She clapped her hands and brushed past me. "Come on!"

She practically ran the whole way. I kept telling her to watch it. All I needed was for her to slip on the muddy trail and hurt herself. When we finally got to the lake's edge, Willow picked up a clump of mud and tossed it in. "What's this lake called?" she asked.

"I don't know," I said. I'd looked on a couple maps, but it was too small to show up. It wasn't much more than a pond, really.

"What do you call it?"

"The lake," I said. Willow rolled her eyes.

"It has to have a name." She looked out over the water and thought for a minute. Then she snapped her fingers. "How about Howling Lake?"

"Howling?"

"Yeah, because of the wolf." She was grinning at me, waiting for me to answer. Howling Lake sounded really stupid to me, but I didn't want to hurt her feelings. Then all of a sudden I remembered the day I'd stood in the same spot and howled my head off. I was glad Willow didn't know about that.

"Sure, okay," I said. "Howling Lake is fine. Want to see where the beavers live?"

There's a beaver lodge at the narrow end of the lake. Willow and I hiked down to take a look at it. It's surrounded by water and looks like a big island made out of sticks and mud. We didn't see any sign of the beavers, except for the million and one birch stumps that were gnawed to a point. I found a real beaver stick and gave it to Willow. She put her camera on a rock and we posed with the beaver lodge in the background and the white beaver stick between us. I made my ugliest face, the one where I pull my cheeks out and push my nose up to look like a pig. Willow jabbed me with her elbow, but it was too late. The camera had already clicked.

We hiked all over that day and ate a ton of snacks. I'd brought some snacks of my own, venison jerky from last year, for starters. Willow loved it until I told her what it was. After that she wouldn't touch it because she said it made her think of eating Bambi, so I ate all the rest. We didn't see any animals, but I did show Willow the pine tree where the bald eagles nest in the summer. She took a couple pictures of the huge messy nest.

As usual, Willow had a million questions. What is that bird called? What kind of tree is that? What do the beavers eat? Can you really walk on the lake when it's frozen? How do the fish breathe if the water is ice? What happens to frogs in the winter? Are baby beavers cute? I answered as many of her questions as I could. It felt good to know so much about the animals and birds and other stuff. I'd spent almost three years hanging around these woods. Now I had someone to tell everything I'd learned on my own. That felt good too.

On top of questions, Willow told me more about her family. She told me the names of all her sisters, Alison, Cara, and Katie, and what their favorite things were (Alison, stuffed rabbits and acting big; Cara, eating and Barbie dolls; Katie, whining and coloring with markers). She told me that her dad is an illustrator (calendars, greeting cards, picture books for little kids) and that her mom is a potter (which I already knew). Then she told me that what her mom really likes to do is sculpt, but it's harder to earn money doing that.

Willow told me about their dogs, Marbles and Millie, and how Tunafish the cat got her name (she climbed up on the counter and ate a whole can of tuna fish when she was a kitten and had diarrhea for two days). It seemed Willow never ran out of things to talk about. That first time we met, when she was so talkative, that time it bugged me. I wasn't used to her then. It was fun listening to her now. And as long as she talked, I didn't have to say anything, unless she asked questions, and then all I had to do was answer maybe one out of five of them. We turned over logs, poked around in bushes, sloshed through swampy spots. We didn't see any signs of a wolf but I wasn't too disappointed.

On our way back I reminded Willow that hunting season was coming in less than a month. "Oh, yeah," she said. "And then we can't go out."

"It's dangerous," I said. "Some people shoot at anything that moves. Some of the hunters drink. And a lot of them don't stay off private property like they're supposed to." There'd been a death in our area last year, a guy shot his own son. Something like that happens every year. I didn't tell Willow about it, though.

"So what do you do during hunting season?"

"I go hunting with Dad," I said. "On our own property."

"That's gross," said Willow. She made a disgusted face. I shrugged. Lots of people think hunting is bad. They can't understand how a person can love nature and still hunt.

"We don't do it for fun," I explained. "We do it for food."

"But doesn't it make you feel *terrible*?"

"Do you feel terrible when you eat pepperoni pizza?"

"No," said Willow with a grin. "I LOVE pizza!"

"Someone had to kill that pig to make the pepperoni."

"Oh, yeah," said Willow. "I forgot about that. But still . . ."

"Sometimes I don't like hunting," I admitted. "It's never nice to watch something die. Dad waits until he has a perfect shot. He's really patient. He usually drops them with a single bullet." Willow shuddered. "I'll tell you something that's worse to see," I said.

"What?"

"A deer that's starving to death. There isn't enough food in the winter for all the deer up here. The wolves take some, people take some, and still there isn't enough food and lots of them starve, especially if the snow gets deep."

"Let's NOT talk about hunting anymore," said Willow.

"Okay. I just want to make sure you don't go out," I said, and I really meant it. "And tell your family too," I added.

"Okay, okay." said Willow.

We were heading back toward the cave along a path we hadn't taken before when we passed through a stand of pine. It smelled great. There wasn't as much underbrush because it's hard for things to grow where pine trees drop their needles, so it was easier to see between the trees. Willow was in front of me on the trail. She had her hood down and her hair was in two floppy ponytails that swished back and forth with each step.

"If I can't go out during hunting season," she said, "I'll be bored to death at home. Hiking around with you is a blast." I felt my face turn bright red. Good thing she couldn't see me right then. I'd already had the exact same thought.

In order to get back to the cave, we had to take a shortcut. I told Willow where to turn off. We had to duck under a fallen tree. We walked for a hundred yards or so. The trail wasn't a good one, but I knew my way around, so I wasn't worried. We came to another fallen log, but it was too low to pass under, so we climbed over. Willow went first, then she reached her hand over to help me. I didn't take it, of course, but I did look down, and when I did I saw something white stuck to the bark. "Check this out," I said. I hopped over the log and squatted down beside it. Willow came close and looked. It was a hunk of white-and-gray fur, not a big hunk but a little clump like Rhonda sheds around the house.

At first neither of us said anything. I pulled the fur off the tree and rubbed it between my fingers. Then I passed half of it over to Willow. "Do you think this is from a wolf?" she asked, but I didn't answer her. I was heading down the trail, looking . . .

searching, *there!* In a spot where there weren't any leaves or pine needles, where the ground was still muddy, I found what I was looking for, a footprint, exactly like a dog's, only huge with spread-out toes. Willow came and squatted next to me. She stared at the spot. "Is it fresh?" she whispered. I nodded.

"It can't be older than a day and a half, because of the rain Friday night. See how even the edges are still damp?" I put my finger into each toe impression. *King.* The king of the north woods. I still hadn't told Willow about naming the wolf. Somehow it felt too private. We squatted there side by side for a long time, and we were so quiet you couldn't even hear us breathe. The wind blew through the tops of the pine trees up above, a chickadee called, and far away a raven cawed. Was the wolf close enough to smell us? Was he out there watching us? The thought made me shiver.

We didn't talk anymore until we got to the cave. I looked down at Willow's house. A couple kids were playing the yard, but I was too far away to tell which ones they were. Willow grabbed my sleeve. "When does hunting season start again?"

"The first weekend in November."

Willow frowned and let go of me and ticked

off numbers on her fingers. "Okay, then we have twenty-six days left to find the wolf."

"Right." Almost four weeks to go. The fact was, there was almost no chance of us seeing the wolf. Wolves aren't stupid. They can smell humans miles away. Maybe we'd scared him. Maybe he'd only passed under that log minutes before us. Whenever we got anywhere near him, he'd take off. That's how it would be. We'd get close, maybe, but that would be it. Just then Willow did something that about made me jump out of my skin. She howled.

It was a super loud howl, and she sounded just like the Wolf Man in the horror movie. "Would you shut up!" I yelled. The sound stopped in midhowl. "You just about gave me a heart attack!"

"I thought if I howled, maybe the wolf would howl back. I read it in a book." She grinned at me and we listened for a second.

"It's long gone," I said. I took a deep breath and hoped Willow wouldn't notice how much she'd really scared me.

"We could go looking a couple times a week," said Willow. "Or more, if you want. We're so close! How about I call you after school tomorrow?"

"Okay," I said. It wouldn't hurt to look around

some more. I touched the fur in my jacket pocket.

"Next time I'll bring some plaster of Paris. My mom has tons of it. Then if we find more footprints, we can make a casting!" Willow sort of bobbed up and down. She was grinning now. "Ooooh, this is SO exciting!" She spun around and one of her ponytails smacked me in the face. "Oh, sorry, sorry," she said, but she was still smiling. She stopped bouncing around and stared at me. She's a tiny bit taller than I am. "You should come over for dinner, Perry Dubwah," she said. I shook my head. "Oh, come on. Everyone will like you. You can tell them about the footprint. Otherwise, they'll think I'm lying. Especially Alison. Please?"

"No, I can't," I said. It wasn't exactly the truth, but it wasn't a lie either. I didn't know what Dad would think about me eating with the Pestalozzi family. Probably it would be no big deal. But I didn't want to. Not then. Not yet. Maybe never. We said good-bye and Willow promised to call me soon. I practically ran all the way home.

That night I ate pork and beans and corn bread with Dad. I was starving and I ate piles and piles of the beans. A couple times I reached into my jeans pocket, just to make sure that the tuft of fur was still there. Once, I tried to start a conversation with Dad. I told him that the beaver lodge looked extra thick. Did he think that meant a super cold winter? He shrugged and said, "I hope so. That'll mean more firewood to sell and lots of plowing." I told him we'd found some fur that looked like wolf fur. I stopped chewing to see what he would say. "It's probably from Joe Dobbs's old husky." He didn't ask to see it.

I went to bed feeling really lonely, even though Dad was out in the other room reading and Rhonda was snoring on the floor beside my bed. I fell asleep hoping more than anything that Willow would call again. I didn't have to wait long.

We went out four times the next week. On Monday, Tuesday, and Thursday, we didn't have much time after school before it started to get dark, but we went as far as we could. On Saturday, after me and Dad got back from town, Willow and I spent the whole afternoon looking for signs of wolves. We found eleven baby pond turtles that had just hatched, a couple eagle feathers, and two genuine beaver sticks beside another pond, but we didn't find any wolves.

The first night, Monday, I tried to get my dad to

talk to me during dinner. Before dinner, I'd actually written down a bunch of questions, hoping something would catch his attention. It was interesting stuff, like "Willow named the lake Howling Lake. What do you think?" or "Did you know that in a pack, the female alpha wolf lifts her leg to pee just like a male?"

"Oh, yeah? No kidding" was all he said. We hadn't talked much for three years. What had changed in me? Why was I thinking up questions? Was it from hearing all of Willow's millions of questions? Was she rubbing off on me? I didn't think so. I'm nothing like her. I only knew that there was this something inside me that wanted Dad to talk to me. I went to bed feeling hungry inside, but it wasn't the kind of hungry that food can fix.

On Monday, Tuesday, and Thursday, I said no when Willow begged me to come have dinner and meet the rest of her family. Saturday morning I got two letters from my mom, one in an orange envelope with a pumpkin sticker and one in plain white. I put them in the sack with all the other letters and made myself forget about them. On Saturday afternoon, when Willow asked me to come over for dinner, I said OK.

CHAPTER
14

Oh, goody, goody, goody!" said Willow when I told her I'd go to her house for dinner. We'd been out for three hours without finding anything, not even an interesting bird. Willow clapped her hands and then put one fist in the air and danced around in a little circle. Her hood flew back and her glasses slipped halfway down her nose.

"Don't get a hernia," I said, feeling my ears turn red. We were up at the cave. The wind had come up and was bitter cold. Maybe if she noticed my red ears, Willow would think it was because of the wind. I didn't have my hat on. She pulled up her hood and cinched it around her face.

"I won't get a hernia," she said sarcastically. "It's just that I bet Alison a dollar that you'd come to-night. YEA!" Her hood was cinched really tight around her face. It made her glasses look huge. I had to work really hard not to smile at how funny she looked. "We're having pizza. Come on!" She spun around and headed toward the house.

"So, did you kill the pig to make pepperoni?" I asked, catching up to her on the steep path. It felt like I had a ball in my stomach.

"Very funny," said Willow. She didn't turn around but she took a step and a skip and I knew she wasn't mad.

When we got to the front porch, I could smell the pizza. Willow smelled it too because she took a deep breath and said, "My mom makes the best pizza." She yanked open the door and we went in. We were immediately surrounded.

Two little dogs started sniffing my boots. They looked like black mops with legs. One jumped up on me. "Down, Millie!" Willow yelled.

"How do you tell them apart?" I asked. By this time all three of Willow's sisters were standing in the hall staring at me.

The little one with red hair answered. "Millie has a littler nose," she said, smiling shyly up at me.

"And she always stinks," said the chubby one with messy ponytails.

"She does not either stink, Cara," said the other

sister, who I figured must be Alison. She scooped Millie the Mop Dog into her arms. "Poor puppy. You don't stink. See?" She shoved the dog in my face. It smelled like a dead rat.

"Knock it off, Alison," said Willow. She'd taken off her coat and hung it on a peg by the door. "Put your coat and junk there, Perry, and don't pay any attention to them."

I took off my coat and boots. Willow's sisters watched everything I did. I felt like some kind of freak. Willow must have noticed. "Would you all just get out of here right *now*?" They moved down the hall a couple feet and stared at me from there. Willow sat on the floor and pulled off her boots. "You are so lucky to be an only child."

"I guess," I said. No way was I about to tell her about my sister. She could think I was really, truly an only child. Still, even though it was technically true, it made me feel weird to be called an only child.

When I had my boots off, we went down the hall and through the living room to the dining room, where the three sisters were now waiting and staring. "Oh, yeah," said Willow, as we passed, "I should introduce you. Alison is the big one,

Cara is the fat one, and Katie is the little one."

"I'm not fat," said Cara.

"I'm not little," said Katie. "Ian is littler than me."

"*You're* Perry Du-BWAH," said Alison.

I gritted my teeth. "It's Du-BOICE," I said, but she didn't hear me. Willow was standing in front of her with one hand held out.

"You owe me a dollar," said Willow.

"I do not. It wasn't a real bet," said Alison. She stuck her tongue out at Willow.

"Liar!"

"*Mom!*" Alison yelled, and then Willow yelled and then I heard another voice yelling from the kitchen.

"That's enough, girls. I've about had it with your fighting!" She came to the doorway with a scowl on her face. Several wisps of long red hair had escaped her ponytail and hung in her face. Her hands were clean this time, but the nails were dirty. She had Ian on one hip. He had pulled her glasses off and had one end of them in his mouth. "Hey! Perry!" said Mrs. Pestalozzi. The scowl disappeared instantly and she smiled. She took the glasses away from Ian. He started to cry.

"Alison owes me a dollar," said Willow.

"Willow called me fat," whined Cara.

"I don't want to hear about it," said Mrs. Pestalozzi. Out of the corner of my eye I saw Alison stick her tongue out at Willow again. Ian was really crying now.

"Nice to see you again, Perry," said Mrs. Pestalozzi, raising her voice above Ian's. "Can you stay for dinner?"

I nodded. "I should call my dad, though," I said. I was sure he wouldn't care. Why would he care? Still, I felt nervous about calling. In all the time since we'd moved, I'd never gone to a friend's house. It felt weird because it wasn't normal for me, that's all.

"Tell him Willow's dad will drive you home afterward. Why don't you stay and play Monopoly after dinner? That's what we do every Saturday night."

"I get the dog," said Alison, raising her hand.

"I get the car," said Cara, jumping up and down.

"*I* want the doggie," said Katie. "You always get the doggie."

"You can't play, Katie." said Willow. "You can't even read yet."

"I CAN TOO READ!" yelled Katie, stomping one foot. Mrs. Pestalozzi rolled her eyes and put Ian down. He made a beeline over to me and put his hands up, like he expected me to pick him up. I moved backward a couple steps. I didn't want to touch him. I bumped into a chair. Where was the phone, anyway? Ian followed me and squatted down in front of me. He poked the end of my sock with a little finger.

"Toesies?" he looked up at me and smiled. Then he pointed to his own bare toes. "Toesies."

"You only memorize books," I heard Cara say. "You can't *read*."

"I can too read!" yelled Katie. "*One fish, two fish, red fish, blue fish, black fish, blue fish, old fish, new fish.*" Katie quoted from the Dr. Seuss book at top speed.

"That's not reading," Cara said triumphantly; "it's memorizing."

"I'm not nemorizing!" Katie wailed.

Ian patted my foot and pointed up at me.

"Berry. Toesics." Why did he have to call me Berry? I swallowed and patted him on the head and wished he would go away. I'm not used to babies. The phone. Where was the stupid phone? I was starting to feel like I'd made a humongous mistake. I wanted to get out of that madhouse.

"Hey, uh, Ian," I said to the baby. "Where's the phone?"

"Tullafome?" he said and headed away from me. How stupid to have to ask a baby where the phone was. This place was crazy.

"If you WANT to stay and play Monopoly, that is," said Mrs. Pestalozzi. She grinned and winked at me. "The phone's over there." I opened my mouth to tell her I didn't need to phone, that I'd just remembered something and had to go. Ian picked up the phone.

"Tullafome!" he yelled. "Tullafome!"

"Hey," said a deep, soft voice. A tall, thin gray-haired man came up behind Mrs. Pestalozzi and put one hand on her shoulder. "Is this the famous Perry Du-BWAH?"

"That's him," said Willow. "Alison owes me a dollar, Dad." I saw Willow's dad's eyes move in her direction but he didn't say anything. Definitely ignoring her. It was pretty funny.

"Hi," I said. Willow's dad wore those clear glasses without frames. His gray eyes crinkled at the corners and his forehead had lines too, like he was surprised a lot. He smiled and his eyebrows went up and he reached out his hand to shake. I stuck out my hand and we shook. His hand was warm and smooth. I noticed blue-and-red paint stains on his fingers.

"Willow talks about you constantly," said Mr. Pestalozzi. "You're quite the celebrity around here." He smiled while he talked and it made those eye crinkles even crinklier. His teeth were big and white and there was a wide space between the two front ones. "We hear you're a regular expert on the outdoors."

"Nah," I said, feeling weird because everyone was staring at me and feeling good because they thought I was an expert. "I just read a lot."

"Berry!" yelled Ian from down below. He put the portable phone down right on my foot and looked up. "Shake hans!" He made a serious face and nodded his dark head up and down so hard that his curls shook. Everyone laughed. Willow's dad patted my shoulder then he scooped Ian upside down into his arms. Ian squealed.

"Nice to have you here, Perry," said Mr. Pestalozzi. "You're welcome anytime."

"Thanks," I said. I could still leave, I thought. But I *was* starving and the pizza smelled incredible. Willow had asked me a bunch of times and I was getting tired of saying no. Once wouldn't hurt. I picked up the phone off my foot and crossed to the little table next to the couch, where it had been before

Ian got hold of it. I punched in our phone number. I looked up while I waited for it to connect and noticed a wooden crucifix hanging on the wall. There was a little silver Jesus on the cross. All of a sudden I got this flashback of Great-grandma Dubois teaching me this prayer called the Hail Mary.

I couldn't have been more than four. I hadn't remembered it before now. Great-grandma said Marie for Mary, because of her French accent. I remembered how old her hands looked, how warm and dry they'd felt around my hands as we touched a string of little blue beads together. That's the first time I remember seeing a Jesus on the cross up close, at the end of that string of beads. Great-grandma kissed him when she was done praying and let me kiss him too. I remember Dad wasn't too thrilled when he found out later. "No religion for my kid, Grandma," he'd said.

"But he's a Catholic," said Great-grandma. "Like all of us."

"Not me, not my kid," said Dad, and that was that. I looked at the Pestalozzis' crucifix and thought of the last time I'd seen one.

There was a huge ivory cross at Livvy's funeral,

high on the wall behind where the priest did all his stuff. The Jesus was different, though. Instead of being dead, like on Great-grandma's little cross or the one here in Willow's living room, he looked alive, with his arms raised up. His eyes were open and he had a smile. I remembered wondering if a statue could see, and feeling stupid afterward for wondering it. Livvy's funeral was the only time I'd ever been in a church. I stared at the telephone base on the table. The phone rang at my house.

The girls were fighting about the Monopoly dog and *One fish, two fish* again. What a loony bin this house is, I thought. They were loud. The phone rang again. I swallowed. It rang again and halfway through the ring the answering machine picked up.

This is Jack Dubois. Leave your name and number after the tone and I'll get back to you. I waited for the beep.

"Hi, Dad," I said, hoping he didn't hear too much of the racket going on in the background. "Willow invited me to stay for dinner and they're having pizza. They'll bring me home later, so don't worry." Willow was now standing right in front of me.

"Monopoly. *Monopoly*," she whispered, jiggling and bouncing up and down.

"I might stay and play Monopoly but I haven't decided yet," I added. Willow frowned at me. I left the phone number and hung up.

"What did he say?" asked Willow.

"It was the answering machine," I said. "I left a message. He's probably out on a delivery."

"I bet you're scared I'll cream you in Monopoly."

"No way," I said. I'd never played Monopoly before, but I wasn't about to tell her that.

"Pizza!" yelled Mrs. Pestalozzi from the kitchen.

"Want to help set the table?" asked Willow. She crossed to a big cabinet and jerked open the door. There were stacks of plastic plates and glasses inside.

"Okay," I said.

"Somebody has to have the thimble," said Cara, who was standing so close she was almost touching me.

"You have the thimble this time, remember?" said Willow. "Would you just get away from Perry, Cara. Jeez. You're in his face."

"It isn't my turn for the thimble," said Cara. She moved about one inch away from me. "I get the dog or the hat."

"Stop talking about that stupid game," said Willow. Just then, Mr. Pestalozzi poked his head out the kitchen door and grinned at me. Ian was on his shoulders.

"It'll be nice to have another man around for Monopoly, Perry," he said. Ian pulled off his dad's glasses and put them on his own face. "I have to warn you, these girls are ruthless." Mr. Pestalozzi winked and gave me the thumbs up. Willow put a stack of plates in my hands.

"I'm *not* taking the thimble," whined Cara.

"Shut up and get the forks, okay?" said Willow.

"You're not the boss of me, Willow," said Cara. "I get the dog."

"I'll take the thimble," I said.

CHAPTER
15

Everyone played Monopoly that night, except for Ian, who had to go to bed at seven. I learned that Monopoly is a game that can go on and on, so after that first night, when we didn't finish the game, Mr. P (that's what I started calling him in my mind) said I'd have to come next Saturday too, and that we'd start up where we left off. We all wrote down how much money we had and how many deeds and houses and hotels. Mr. P took me home at nine and came up on the porch to meet Dad. I was a little nervous about that, since people don't usually stop by to visit and also because I'd only left a message. I didn't know what Dad would think about my being out so late with people he didn't know.

I petted Rhonda while the two men shook hands and introduced themselves. Mr. P said he'd heard about Dad's business and that he'd be needing some firewood soon. That got Dad's attention but it's not like he was friendly or smiled or anything. My dad is not what you'd call a people person. He said he'd bring a load by anytime, just to let him know when.

Right before he left, Mr. Pestalozzi stood by his car door and said they'd really enjoyed having me over. Dad nodded and looked at me. "You've got a nice boy there, Jack," said Mr. P, and I felt my face turn red. I bent over to tighten the laces on my boot.

"He's a good kid," said Dad. "Smart too." How weird, I thought. Dad sounds proud. It's just that it wasn't a normal thing for my dad to say, that's all. I mean, I knew he knew I got good grades and stuff, but I'd never heard him actually say it. I felt my mouth pull itself into a smile. Rhonda licked my face.

The next Saturday at the Pestalozzis', we had waffles for dinner and Monopoly afterward. Willow started calling it the Great Monopoly War. The Saturday after that we had hamburgers, which me and Willow and Mr. P made. I finally managed to get both Park Place and Boardwalk and then I started to clean up.

Mrs. Pestalozzi was the banker. The funny part is she wasn't very businesslike at all. She was always giving money away. Like, if you were down to your last five-dollar bill and you had to pay something, she'd slip you a fifty. She did it to everyone. That's another reason the game never ended. No one lost, and no one really won. It was a blast. Actually, it wasn't the game that was a blast. Monopoly is only fun when you're winning. What was so fun was being with Willow's family, even when they were fighting, which was most of the time.

They didn't make a big deal about me after that first night. It was like I'd always been around them. The third time I was over, Alison tried to pick a fight with me. I told her to shut up and no one even blinked. For an instant I wondered if I would have had fights with Olivia, brother and sister stuff where you tell each other to shut up. I didn't know and I would never know. This sounds weird, but having a fight with Alison felt sort of good.

Right up until hunting season, Willow and I looked for the wolf on Saturday afternoons. We went a few times after school, but the days were getting really short and we didn't have much time. Twice Mrs. Pestalozzi made us bring Alison and Cara, but we didn't show them the cave. They hiked OK for little kids, except for all their bickering.

We didn't see or hear anything, but we did find a big footprint one of the days and made a plaster cast of it. I don't know if it was really a wolf or just a dog footprint, but I have it in my room and it's awesome either way just because it *might* be a wolf print. We found that print just in time, too. It snowed a couple inches two days before hunting season opened, and I could tell by the looks of it that this snow would stay. Winter comes early in the north woods.

Once hunting started, Willow and I didn't go on any more hikes. In fact, I didn't go far from home at all unless I was in a car. Even on our own property I wore a bright orange hat when I went out, and I didn't let Rhonda get out of my sight. Dad has No Trespassing/No Hunting signs all around our property, but some people don't pay any attention to signs. I missed going out hiking, but I figured King was long gone. It was sort of sad. Sometimes when I thought about it, I wondered if I'd imagined hearing him, or if I'd only heard a coyote or some weird bird. Anyway, with all those guns going off, and all the hunters in the woods, it wasn't too likely that a wolf would hang around; if there was a wolf, that is. I was starting to think we'd imagined the whole thing.

Dad got a six-point buck the first morning of hunting season. How's that for luck? I helped him clean it and cut up the meat to go in the freezer. He said I could have the hide. I got a book at the library on leather and decided to tan the hide and make something cool with it.

Those three Saturdays during hunting season, Dad dropped me off in the afternoon at the Pestalozzis' on the way home from town. Sometimes we did stuff in the house. Cara always wanted to play Barbies, but no way would I agree to that. Alison has a million Legos. I'm pretty good at Legos. We had a spaceship-building contest and Willow said I won. I think she won. Her spaceship had a computer with buttons that worked.

One of the Saturdays, Mrs. Pestalozzi let me and Willow make little pots out of some leftover clay. First we made these long clay snakes. Then we wound them around and around on themselves to make a pot shape. That week Mrs. Pestalozzi fired them in her kiln and we got to glaze them. I made mine sky blue. It's on my bookshelf, right next to the footprint.

One weekend we got a huge dump of snow, so

Dad and I didn't make it to town. Dad had to plow for the county, so on his way out to pick up the big snowplow from the county garage he dropped me off at the Pestalozzis'. Me and Willow and all the other kids played in the snow. Mr. P helped us build a fort in their yard. You should have seen him. He grew up in California and he hasn't been around snow much. He acted just like a kid! He even made these huge snow angels. Willow took a picture of him doing it.

Whenever I was at the Pestalozzis' Ian hung around me constantly. Willow said it was because he looks up to me, since I'm a guy. At first he made me really nervous. He kept wanting me to pick him up, or if I was sitting someplace, he'd try to climb into my lap. Sometimes his hands and face were really gross, all covered with peanut butter or spaghetti sauce, but that's not what made me nervous. I mean, a guy like me can clean a deer and not get grossed out. Kid messes aren't that big a deal. It's just that I kept thinking of Livvy. She had blonde hair, and she wasn't chubby like Ian, but babies are babies.

For a long time I hadn't thought of her hardly at all. Now every time I was at the Pestalozzis' house, I was reminded of babies and babies reminded me of her. It's hard to explain. Sticky hands, pacifiers, baby shampoo smell, slobbering, all that stuff brought back memories. After a while I got used to being around Ian and the memories didn't seem like such a big deal. I even started letting him sit on my lap, except when his diapers hung low with a load of poop. Jeez. Babies stink a mile away when they're like that.

Every Saturday after dinner, after Ian was in bed and all the dishes were washed, we'd play Monopoly. Sometimes we'd fight, but mostly we had a good time. Katie always had to sit by me. She'd pull her chair real close and sort of lean toward me until she was practically on my lap. "Would you get *away*?" Willow would crab.

"She's okay," I'd say. I got used to Katie too.

I got used to hanging out with people who make a lot of noise. I got used to all the interrupting, the fighting, the sniffling noses. I got used to smelling a fart and having everyone giggle and blame it on me, even when I didn't do it. I got used to hearing Katie scream when she couldn't have the dog in Monopoly and then Willow yelling "Oh, just GROW UP!" over the top of the screaming. I got used to Cara complaining she was hungry all the time. I got in a couple more fights with Alison.

I got used to helping with dishes and grating cheese for pizza and watching Mr. P try to scrub the paint off his hands before dinner. And I started thinking about a bunch of things.

First of all, I started thinking that the whole home school thing was pretty dumb. Other kids went to school and did stuff like spelling bees and recess and math team. I'd be hot on a math team. I hadn't wanted to go to school, not once I got used to being home all the time with Dad. Now I felt differently. I liked doing stuff with other kids, even if they were girls. It didn't seem fair to have to stay home all the time. But how could I tell my dad that?

The other thing is I started wondering how a house that wasn't my house could feel so much like home. Every chance I got, I hung out at the Pestalozzis'. Dad didn't seem to care if I was around or not. He seemed quieter than ever before. Was he mad at me for having friends? Was he sad that I wasn't around all the time? Was it my fault he was so quiet? Had he always been this quiet and I just never noticed? One night he stayed up super late reading through a big pile of papers that had come in the mail in a manila envelope. He stopped asking me about my schoolwork. Something was happening, and I wasn't sure what. Whatever it was, I worried it was my fault. My house didn't feel like home. Maybe it never had. I felt guilty having so much fun with the Pestalozzis, but not guilty enough to stop.

The Thursday right after hunting season ended was Thanksgiving. Mrs. Pestalozzi said me and Dad would be welcome to have turkey with them. I thought it was a great idea, but Dad said he had six requests for wood that week and had to work. Thanksgiving Day I helped Dad split wood and load the truck. Oh, we had a turkey dinner all right, the little frozen roast-in-a-box kind that makes its own gravy. And we watched a football game together. I made popcorn. Big deal. All day Friday I split wood with Dad, wondering what the Pestalozzis were doing on their day off, wishing I didn't care so much that I didn't know.

The next day, Saturday, I had this brainstorm. I decided to stay home instead of going to the Pestalozzis', even though I really wanted to see them. Maybe Dad was missing me. Maybe he didn't like me spending so much time with another family. It was snowing hard when Dad and I left for Grand Marais. I told Dad that I didn't feel like going anywhere that afternoon and not to drop me off at the Pestalozzis' on the way home from town. All he did was nod and say, "Okay."

When we got to town, instead of going to the post office, I asked Dad to drop me off at the drugstore. I bought a pack of playing cards with grizzly bears on the picture side. My brilliant plan was to ask Dad if he wanted to play gin rummy after dinner (I learned it from Willow). When Dad picked me up, there was a letter with my name on it lying on the truck seat. I stuffed it in my back pocket and made myself quit thinking about it.

Willow was bummed when I called. "But it's Italian sausage pizza, your *favorite*." I could tell she was sad by the sound of her voice. "You couldn't come for Thanksgiving, and you couldn't come yesterday, and I'm going bonkers with all these little kids. And what about the Great Monopoly War? Mom said everyone gets a thousand dollar bonus this week, for keeping our rooms clean." I felt my shoulders droop. I slouched down onto the couch. I wanted to go like crazy. Rhonda groaned at my feet. I scratched her ear with my toe.

"I have to stay home," I said. "I've got stuff to do."

"Are you grounded?"

"No way," I said. Willow and her sisters were always getting in trouble for doing things. They couldn't believe that I never got in trouble. I don't think they could understand that there's such a thing as a kid who makes SURE he doesn't get in trouble. That's me.

I didn't want to talk to her for very long. Talking to her made me want to go over there too much. *This is my home,* I told myself. *Dad is my family.* So I said I had to go and hung up. Because of the snow, Dad plowed all afternoon. When he came home I had pancakes ready for our dinner. I think Dad was surprised I'd thought of making dinner like that, without him asking me or anything. His eyebrows went up when I told him.

"What kind of syrup do you want?" I asked. I'd heated up both blueberry and maple.

"Blueberry," said Dad. "Thanks." I passed him the little pitcher and he poured syrup on his stack of pancakes.

"So, Dad, I was just wondering," I stabbed a big hunk of pancake, "do you like to play cards?"

"Sometimes," said Dad. His mouth was full. "How come?"

"Oh, I just thought it would be fun to play a

game. I bought some cards today." I pulled the grizzly cards out of my pocket and laid them on the table. "The Pestalozzis play Monopoly every Saturday night, but I'm kind of tired of that game. Maybe you and I could play something else." Dad looked at my cards and frowned.

"Sure, we could play sometime," said Dad. "But as soon as I finish eating I have to go plow. Looks like it might be an all-nighter." An all-nighter is when it snows steadily all night. The guys who plow drive up and down the roads, keeping them as clear as possible during the storm. It cuts down on accidents, and it's easier than waiting and having to plow a big load off the roads. Dad got himself three more pancakes. I put the cards back in my pocket. They made a big lump and poked me in the butt.

I felt a big lump someplace else, namely, my throat. I swallowed it down. Big deal, I told myself. So what if you missed a night at the Pestalozzis'? So what if Dad has to plow? It's his job. I gulped down some milk. I can work on that deer hide, I told myself.

"Did you get your letter?" asked Dad. I nodded. He kept looking at me. He even stopped chewing. Then he started chewing again, but he was still looking at me and after he swallowed he said, "What do you do with those letters from your mom, anyway, Perry? I've never seen you open one."

His question just about knocked me off my chair. I was so stunned I had to take another big gulp of milk so I wouldn't choke on my food. After all this time, he was asking me about Mom's letters. Why? And what was I supposed to say? If I said "I read them," it would be a lie. But then if I said "I just keep them," it might make him mad.

I'd always been sort of scared to read them, scared that Dad wouldn't approve or something. Dad never talked about Mom. Never *ever*. This was the closest he'd ever come. Wasn't he mad at her anymore? Did he know that I had a huge sack full of letters? If I'd had the guts I would have thrown them all away just to prove I didn't miss her, just to prove I was strong like him. All of this junk went through my head in a flash.

"I save them," I said and stabbed another pancake. Then he asked me the question that made me feel instantly too full to take another bite.

"So, how's she doing?"

"Good," I said quickly, too quickly. Could he tell I was lying?

"She sound happy to you?"

"I guess."

"That's good," said Dad quietly. "She was never happy with me."

I swirled my pieces of pancake around in the syrup with my fork. I stared at my plate and lifted a piece of pancake to my mouth in slow motion. My stomach felt so sick that if I put another bite of pancake in there I knew I might barf. I did it anyway. I chewed the pancake. I felt my dad's eyes on me. I felt the letter that was still in my back pocket.

"I got some stuff from her lawyer," said Dad.

I stabbed another piece of pancake. I tried to pick it up but it fell off my fork. I stabbed it again.

"She wants to see you. You want to go see her?"

"No," I said. Tears blurred my vision. I blinked them away. I stared at the puddle of syrup on my plate. "Do I have to?"

"No," said Dad. "Not if you don't want to." He pushed himself away from the table. "Good pancakes," he said. "Leave the dishes for me." Two minutes later he was out the door.

CHAPTER
16

I worked on the deer hide for about an hour, softening it up, planning how I'd cut it, but I was so restless inside, so full of mixed-up feelings and thoughts that I could hardly concentrate. At seven-thirty I let Rhonda out. It was still snowing, big flakes coming straight down. There wasn't even a whisper of wind and it wasn't that cold. I checked the temp. Twenty-five degrees. Rhonda went around and squatted in her favorite spots. Then all of a sudden she stood straight up and started barking.

"Quiet," I told her, and she looked at me and whined. I was freezing with the door open like that. "Hurry up and get in," I said, but she ignored me, which is unusual for a trained dog like Rhonda. I figured she must not be done with her business and shut the door to give her more time. I leaned up against the door with my forehead pasted to the cold glass. The snow was thick, like falling feathers. I bet there were already eight or nine inches of new snow, and it didn't look like it was going to stop anytime soon. Dad wouldn't be home until morning. I closed my eyes. The window felt good against my face, like a cool, smooth stone.

Her lawyers sent him some stuff. Did I want to visit? No. Yes. No. *No!* Her lawyers must have sent him stuff lots of times before. I'd never thought of that. Why was I hearing about it now? Why was he asking me now if I wanted to visit her? Did she ask before? Did he tell her no without asking me? I kicked the door so hard it hurt my toes. It doesn't matter one bit, I told myself. Not one little teeny bit. I didn't need her. She didn't need me. Maybe her new husband had other kids. Maybe they'd have a baby together.

Why hadn't Dad talked about her before?

I thought about my cave. It had been weeks since I'd hung out in it by myself. Months! Before Willow came, I'd spent at least three or four days a week there, thinking, listening, being alone. I hadn't been to the cave at all during hunting season, and before that, I'd spent so much time hiking around with Willow or doing stuff at her house that I hadn't had much reason to go there, except for meeting Willow before our hikes. Now I wanted to go, just for an hour. If I had to be alone with all of these swirling gut-wrenching feelings, I wanted it to be in my own place, not in this house that felt so empty. I hurried to my room and dug my snowshoes out of the closet.

It didn't take me long to get ready. When I had everything I needed, long johns, turtleneck, fleece sweatshirt, jeans, snow pants, parka, flashlight, I pulled my boots on and went out to the porch. Rhonda was waiting for me. Her back was covered with snowflakes. I strapped on my snowshoes, pulled on my two-layer mittens, grabbed my poles, and took off. Rhonda must have known where we were going. She headed toward the cave without even being told.

The snowshoes were awkward for only a couple minutes. Soon I had the rhythm of snowshoeing down and was going at a pretty good pace. See, you don't walk in a regular way with them or you'd step on them and trip. You have to swing your legs out a bit. Not everyone uses poles, but I like to. I can go faster that way, and I went fast. I was in a hurry. I don't know why the feeling was so strong, but I just had to get to my cave. I started to sweat because of all those clothes. Still, I didn't want to take anything off. I didn't want to risk getting chilled.

Even though it was dark out, the snow was so white that I could see fine, and the path to my cave was so familiar that it didn't take me much longer than normal to get there. I took the flashlight out of my pocket. My heart was racing, mostly because of snowshoeing, but there was this part of me that was pretty nervous about going into the cave at night. I'd never done it before. I'd thought about it and even asked Dad once if I could camp there overnight, but he'd said no. I was pretty sure no animals ever used it, but I hadn't been there for a while and you never know. I shined the light into the dark cave entrance. All I saw was the wood-pile and the fire ring. I let out a big sigh of relief and went in. I took off my parka and made a fire.

I messed with the fire for a long time. I wanted to get it going really well. I stacked and rearranged the wood so it would be in the best position to burn. Then once the logs caught on fire, I poked around in the flames with a stick. I added more wood. By this time, the cave was warm enough, but I wanted more fire, more light. It was so dark! I kept adding wood. There was a layer of hot coals at the bottom, and I stirred and blew on those to get the whole thing hotter. I stared at the flames and listened to the quiet crackle of the logs as they burned. The wood was dry, and the fire didn't smoke much. The draft in the cave sucked the little bit of smoke right out. I got so warm I stripped down to just my jeans and long johns shirt. I laid my jacket, snow pants, and sweatshirt on the ground and sat cross-legged by the fire. Rhonda slept behind me.

I watched the fire. My caveman animals watched me from the shadows. I wondered what the Pestalozzis were doing down in their warm, noisy house. I thought about my dad, plowing up and down the silent, snowy roads in the dead of night. I wondered if he was thinking about Mom too. My eyes burned. My eyelids felt heavy. I leaned against Rhonda and closed them tight.

I'm sitting on a hard rock, but now it's a slippery chair. I'm wearing a little hospital gown that ties in the back, like the one Mom has on under her robe. Dad is squatting next to me and he has one arm around me. Mom comes toward me with a bundle in her arms. Now the bundle is in my lap. It's warm and heavy. Mom looks at me. Her smile is so big it gives her dimples on both sides.

"What do you think, Per Bear?" she asks.

Now I'm at my grandma's house and no one is talking. I'm watching TV. Grandma says it's too loud. I look at her and she's crying. Aunt Stephie is home from college and she's crying too, crying without making any sound. They sniffle a lot. Bugs Bunny smiles at Elmer Fudd. "EH, WHAT'S UP, DOC?" And he whacks him over the head with a bunch of carrots. Aunt Stephie is crying out loud now but I can't turn the TV up or Grandma will scold. I want to get inside the TV with Bugs. "YOU'RE A BAD, BAD WABBIT!" My aunt Stephie says, "Jennie said Jack won't talk to her. He can't stop blaming her." Grandma says, "Shhhh," and points at me, and then they hug. Suddenly I am all alone in the dark but I can still hear them crying, and then it turns into my mom crying and I want to run away, but my legs are frozen to the floor.

Rhonda poked me in the back with her nose and whined, and I woke up. I was sweating but I couldn't stop shivering. I squeezed my eyes shut and rubbed them, erasing the pictures that lingered from the nightmare. I got up and put on my sweatshirt and snow pants, then my jacket. What a stupid idea to come here, I thought angrily. How could I fall asleep? I zipped my jacket up to my chin. Why couldn't I get warm? What time was it anyway? I had to get home. Rhonda stood over by the entrance and whined again.

"Let's go, Rhonda," I said. I grabbed one of my snowshoes and stepped through the entrance to get a scoop of snow to put out the fire. That's when I heard it. I froze. The notes were long and clear, and close by. The sound pierced the darkness. It made the hair on the back of my neck stand up. Rhonda growled.

The wolf howled again and again and I held my breath to listen. I heard another howl, or thought I did. It was faint, far away, or at least it sounded far away. But snow muffles sound. It was probably a lot closer than it seemed. The second howl was different, lower, sadder. It could have come from the same wolf, or it could be that there were more than one. I listened for a long time, until all I could hear was my own heartbeat and the sound of a million tiny snowflakes landing like grains of salt on the ground.

I leaned against the rocks. My heart sounded like bongo drums. *Thup-a, thup-a, thup-a.* The wolf was close. Were there two?

Too close. I tried to swallow but I couldn't. *Wolves never attack people.*

My mouth was dry. My tongue stuck to the roof of my mouth. Rhonda turned around and around in circles. I knelt down and hugged her. I was all alone in the woods and there were wolves out in the night. I fought back the tears that tried to sneak into my eyes.

I had no idea what time it was, no idea how long I'd slept. What an idiot for falling asleep! If Dad came home and I wasn't there—I could only imagine his reaction. I'd seen him get really mad plenty of times in my life, but before it was never at me. He was going to kill me! If I could just get to the Pestalozzis', I thought, I could call home from there, leave a message. I could stay overnight with them. Then I remembered the wolf and knew I couldn't do it. Even though I knew in my head that wolves don't attack people, I was too scared to step foot outside the cave.

The fire. At least I had that and lots of wood. I hurried over to the woodpile and grabbed three big logs. Two white beaver sticks poked up behind the woodpile. They were the same ones I'd picked clean when we first came. I grabbed those too. I dumped the logs on the smoldering coals and arranged them so they'd catch fire. Soon they were blazing, but I couldn't get warm. I sat close, all bundled up in my winter clothes, and poked the fire with the sticks. Rhonda lay at the cave entrance, quiet but alert.

I stayed awake all night, poking at the fire, adding more wood when it died down, trying to get warm, listening, thinking, staring at the flames, worrying about Dad, wondering about the wolf, shivering because I couldn't get warm no matter how the fire blazed. All those times I'd felt lonely before were nothing compared to this. My cave had always been my hideout, my safe place. Now it felt like prison. There was nothing to do but wait until morning. Nothing to do except keep the fire alive.

I found Willow's book of drawings and looked at the wolf she'd made. Then I snapped one of the white beaver sticks in half and burned one end. When I wasn't stoking the fire or adding wood, I drew on the walls of my cave with the stick.

Sometime in the night it quit snowing. As soon as the first hint of dawn peeked into the cave, I tossed the two little stubs that were all that was left of my white beaver sticks into the fire, plopped a big scoop of snow down on the whole thing, strapped on my snowshoes, and headed down the hill to the Pestalozzi house.

Nine silent soot wolves watched me leave.

CHAPTER
17

It was barely light out. There was at least a foot and a half of new snow. Good thing I'd worn my snow-shoes. I shushed through the snow and Rhonda leaped through the drifts like a maniac. I got to the Pestalozzis' back door and knocked. A light was on in the kitchen. I was out of breath from hurrying. My hands itched inside my mittens. Mr. P's face appeared in the window and then the door swung open.

"Thank God!" he said, pushing the storm door against the new load of snow. He turned his head and called into the kitchen. "It's Perry!" The door wouldn't open. I scooped the snow out of the way with my arms and finally pulled it open enough to squeeze through. I stepped inside and Mr. P put his arms around me and gave me a quick hug. "Where've you been, buddy?" he asked. His forehead was wrinkled with concern. He was wearing a blue bathrobe. It felt so good to see someone that I wanted to hug him back, but I didn't. I felt that choking feeling in my throat. Hugging him would have made it worse. I stood there not saying anything, covered with snow, dripping on the floor. By that time, Willow and her mom were standing there in their bathrobes, staring at me, until Willow pushed her way past her dad and grabbed my shoulders. She shook me so hard I thought my head would snap off.

"Oh, Perry Dubwah," she said, half sobbing. "I thought you were dead." I pulled away from her and took off my hat.

"Well, I'm not dead," I said, "and you're getting snow all over yourself. I've got to call my dad." I had to concentrate so my voice wouldn't shake. How come I was feeling this way? Hunger? Was it because of being awake all night?

"He called about four in the morning," said Mrs. Pestalozzi. Her red hair hung in two limp braids on either side of her face. "He wanted to know if we'd seen you at all."

"We told him no," said Mr. P. "He sounded really worried, said he was going to call the sheriff."

I felt my stomach sink to my feet. "That's all we knew until now."

"We've been up ever since your dad called," said Willow. "We couldn't go back to sleep. We heard the wolf last night," said Willow. "We heard him!"

"About ten o'clock," said Mr. P. "I got the girls up and we all sat and listened. We had no idea you were missing."

"I wasn't missing," I said. "I went to the . . . hide-out, that's all. For fun."

"I knew it!" said Willow. She glanced at her dad. "I told Dad about the cave. I told him maybe you went there, but he said there was no way you could have gone that far in deep snow. We didn't even *think* of snowshoes, you know, because we're from California. Oh, *Perry*. How could you be so stupid?"

"I don't know." I pulled my mitten off. How could I tell them the real reason I'd gone out? How could they even begin to understand? I felt dizzy. I wanted to sit down. The cave wasn't a secret anymore, but how could I be mad at Willow for telling? "I heard the wolf from inside the cave," I said, and my voice cracked a little. "I was too scared to go out." I had to call Dad. "Can I please use the phone?"

I stripped off my snow pants and went into the

living room. Willow and her mom and dad followed me. I sank down into the couch and picked up the phone. It shook in my hand. I was so dead tired I could hardly think straight. And I was scared. Scared of what my dad was going to do. I dialed my number. The answering machine picked up. I left a message. I hung up and sat there, the phone in my hand. Willow sat next to me, so close we were touching. I didn't care. I leaned my head back against the couch. I had to reach Dad. After three minutes or so passed, I punched the redial button. The answering machine picked up again.

I spent the next hour redialing my house every five minutes. Mrs. Pestalozzi offered me some toast but I said no. Willow sat next to me and for once, she didn't say a word. Mr. P brought a blanket and covered me. He must have seen me shaking. I didn't care. Every five minutes I punched that redial button.

Until my dad finally answered the phone.

CHAPTER
18

Ten minutes later I heard our big truck pull into the driveway. I was ready to go with all my winter clothing on, waiting in the kitchen. All the kids were up now, and they were quiet. Even Ian didn't beg to be picked up. As soon as I heard the truck I bolted out the back door, grabbed my snowshoes and poles, and trudged through the deep snow around to the front of the house. Rhonda followed close behind me. Dad didn't get out of the truck. He didn't look at me as I tossed my junk in the back and waited for Rhonda to hop in. He didn't even turn his head as I opened the passenger-side door and climbed in. He didn't speak until we were half-way home.

"I've been driving up and down the back roads for hours," he said. "I must have called half the county." I glanced sideways and licked my lips.

I swallowed. Dad's face was white. His cheeks twitched. "Where were you?"

"In my cave," I said. Above the roar of the truck engine, my voice sounded like a whisper. I wanted to tell him everything. I wanted to tell him how scared I'd been, how worried that he'd be mad. I couldn't make myself open my mouth. Dad didn't say anything else. I wished I could crawl under the seat or hide in the glove compartment. I wanted to roll down the window and jump headfirst into a deep snowdrift. I leaned against the door, my face flat up against the cold, cold window.

He didn't start yelling until we were in the house. I'd just pulled off my boots, thinking maybe I'd been stupid to worry about him being mad. Sure, he'd sounded upset in the truck when he'd asked me where I'd been, but upset isn't the same as mad. Not always.

"Do you have any idea what you put me through?" He stood above me, with his hands on his hips. His voice was loud, and I could tell he was holding back.

"I'm sorry, Dad," I squeaked. He was so big that way, with me sitting on the floor and him standing.

"*Sorry?*" he shouted. I was afraid to move, to get up off the floor. "I come home after plowing all night, and the lights are all on and you aren't in your bed, what am I supposed to think? *How could you do this to me?*"

"Please, Dad, I can explain what happened—"

"SHUT UP!" Dad shoved me with his foot. "GET OFF THE FLOOR, MISTER." I scrambled to my feet and he grabbed me by the arm. "DON'T YOU EVER LEAVE THIS HOUSE WITHOUT TELLING ME AGAIN." His fingers dug into the muscle. It hurt like crazy. Tears filled up my eyes, but it wasn't because of the pain. I opened my mouth to apologize some more. That's what I meant to do, anyway. I don't know why I said what I said next.

"HOW CAN I TELL YOU ANYTHING WHEN YOU'RE NEVER AROUND?" I shouted back. I felt the blood filling up my head like it was a balloon. My eyes hurt so much I wanted to squeeze them shut. I stared at my dad instead.

The words were out. I couldn't take them back. I was dead meat.

Dad blinked and frowned at me. He was still holding my arm tight. He pulled me close, up and toward his face, until my face was a couple inches away from his. I made myself look into his furious eyes. I didn't look away. Suddenly, Dad let go and turned away. I fell backward and banged my head on the wall. Dad crossed the room and stood in front of the fireplace, both hands gripping the mantel. I rubbed my head and bit my lip so hard I tasted blood. *I will not cry.* I stood up.

"I went to my cave because I didn't like being home alone," I said. Dad didn't move. "I thought I heard the wolf. I was scared to come out." My voice shook and cracked. Dad didn't move. He didn't turn around. Was he even listening? Finally he spoke.

"My only kid out in a storm God-knows-where, maybe lying in a snowbank dead. That's what I thought. That you might be *dead.*" The last word was no more than a whisper.

Suddenly I wanted to run over to him, put my arms up like Ian does to Mr. P. I wanted to tell him I was glad to be home, that I'd worried all night about him being worried about me, that I'd called as soon as I could. I wanted to tell him over and over again that I was sorry, sorry for leaving without letting him know, sorry for staying out all night, sorry for scaring him, sorry for yelling at him. *Sorry, sorry, sorry. It's all my stupid fault.* But I couldn't. I knew he wouldn't want to hear any of that. Besides, my tongue was glued to the inside of my mouth. My feet were glued to the floor.

Dad stood up straight and turned around. His jaw muscles were tight. He looked at me for a second or two. It made me wish I could shrink away to nothing. "You're grounded," said Dad. "For a month."

My chin twitched. My throat hurt. A month! At the end of a month it would be almost January. In January and February it would be too cold to go to the cave, too cold to hike. I stumbled to my room without saying a word, shut the door, and flopped down on my bed. I didn't bother to change my clothes. I didn't even get under the covers. I pressed my face into the pillow so hard it hurt. It didn't take long for me to fall into a dead sleep.

Dad is yelling at me, screaming in my face. "HOW COULD YOU DO THIS TO ME?" His face is huge. His mouth is like a cave. All of a sudden I shrink down to rat size and I'm way up high looking down and I can see that Dad isn't yelling at me at all. He's yelling at Mom, yelling in her face. "HOW COULD YOU DO THIS TO ME?" he shouts.

"I'm sorry," she says, "I'm leaving." She picks up her purse from a chair. "I'm leaving now."

I WOKE UP with a jerk. I felt as cold as a piece of cement. I turned over onto my back, pulling the quilt up to my chin and snuggling into its softness. Thinking about that dream made me feel sick. Plus, I was totally starving to death. It was dark out, so I figured I'd slept the whole day. That's when it hit me that Dad must have covered me up. It was his quilt, the big one off his bed. Grandma Dubois made it for him when he graduated from high school. I pulled the old quilt up over my head and lay there in the darkness, trying to get warm, trying to get that dream out of my head. I didn't want to see Dad, even if he had covered me with his quilt. If I could have stayed in my room for another day, I would have. The problem was, I had to pee. Finally I got up my nerve and got out of bed. My clothes felt gross after sleeping in them. I opened my bedroom door. Rhonda jumped up and put her front paws on my shoulders. She licked my face.

"Knock it off," I said, pushing her down. I looked around. I listened. I looked outside. It was snowing hard again. And Dad was gone.

Me and Rhonda spent a lot of days alone after that. It snowed way more than usual for late fall, which meant lots of plowing and lots of people who wanted firewood. The Pestalozzis called for a load. Dad said I could go with him to deliver it if I wanted, but I said no. I didn't want to see them. It would have reminded me too much of all the fun I'd had with them, and how lonely I was now. And I didn't want to be cooped up in the truck with Dad. I didn't want to be with anyone except Rhonda. I didn't need anyone. Day after day I worked on my schoolwork, split and loaded firewood when Dad asked for help, read books, and watched TV.

Willow had called the day after Dad grounded me. I told her I was grounded for a month. "A month?" she'd squealed into the phone. "Clear until Christmas? That's horrible!"

"I guess," I'd said. I didn't want to talk about it. I didn't want to talk to her. Talking to her made me have to bite the inside of my cheek. I didn't want people calling me. Before Willow came, I didn't know what I was missing. Now I knew; boy, did I ever know what I was missing. I didn't want to be reminded of it.

"Uh, I gotta go, Willow. See you around," I'd said.

Every time she called I said I had to go, but she didn't get the hint and kept calling. Finally I did something I would never have thought I'd do. I lied to her. I told her I wasn't allowed phone calls while I was grounded and that if she didn't stop calling me I'd be grounded forever. She didn't call after that.

After blowing up at me and grounding me for a month, Dad didn't act mad anymore. In fact, he actually seemed almost friendly for a few days, trying harder or something, like when he asked if I wanted to go with him to take the wood to the Pestalozzis' house. Maybe he was feeling guilty for being so mad. I don't know. It wasn't like him, that's for sure. Two nights after he grounded me he asked me about schoolwork, but not just the regular questions.

"So, tell me about that book you're reading these days, Perry," he said during dinner. We were eating fried chicken. It tasted like crumbly salted grease. "Is it about wolves?"

I shook my head. "Volcanoes," I said. Usually, a talk between my dad and me would end right there, but not this time.

"Dobbs says that he's heard the wolf a couple times." He looked at me like he was expecting me to say something. I didn't say anything. "Think we ought to report it to someone?"

How many times before had I wished he would ask me about the wolf? Now it felt fake. He was trying too hard. He couldn't just ground me for a month and then try to act like nothing had happened. I didn't answer his question about reporting the wolf. I swallowed a big crusty bite of chicken that I hadn't chewed well enough. It scratched my throat so bad it brought tears to my eyes. Dad didn't say anything else during dinner.

A couple days later Dad said he had a delivery up near the border. Did I want to go? I said no thanks. I couldn't tell if the look on his face was mad or disappointed. He left at eight that morning and didn't come back until dark. He asked me two other times that week, but I always said no, and he didn't ask anymore after that. The weird thing is when he stopped asking me to go with him, it felt awful.

After a while, each day being grounded started to feel exactly like another. I slept late some days, worked on school, hung around, sometimes not even changing out of my pajamas until lunchtime. If Dad noticed the pajamas, he didn't say anything.

After his attempts at being friendly, he pretty much left me alone. Math was getting harder. It wasn't making sense like it had before, so I quit doing it, gave myself a break. I didn't say anything to Dad. I knew he could have helped me, if I'd asked. My dad is good at math. But I didn't ask for help and pretty soon I was behind.

I thought about Willow and her family all the time. At first I'd tried erasing them from my brain, but for some reason the erasing thing wasn't working as well as it used to. During the day I wondered what Mr. and Mrs. Pestalozzi were up to. At night I wondered what they were all having for dinner. On Saturday nights, when I knew they were playing Monopoly without me, I went right to my room after dinner and didn't come out until morning.

I had a hard time falling asleep. And when I did fall asleep, I had bad dreams, the kind that make you wake up feeling like you haven't slept at all, the kind that make your head hurt and your body ache. It made me dread bedtime, even though I kept telling myself that dreams are nothing to be scared of. Some nights I'd have one bad dream and then I'd wake up for a while, then I'd go back to sleep and have another bad dream. A lot of mornings I woke up feeling exhausted.

I thought I heard the wolf twice while I was grounded, both times at night when I couldn't sleep or was in between nightmares. I decided it was really juvenile to give a wolf a name, so I stopped thinking of the wolf as King. A wolf is nothing but a big wild dog. But wolves are free and it made me feel jealous thinking about them. Both times I heard the howling I put my pillow over my head to shut out the sound, but even with the pillow pressed against my ears, I heard the howling. Whether it was from outside, from the real wolves, or from inside my own head, I couldn't tell for sure. It didn't matter anyway. Not anymore.

CHAPTER
19

Three weeks went by. I woke up around noon one day and remembered it was Sunday. One more week to go. Dad was sitting at the kitchen table with a cup of coffee. He looked up when he heard me. I went to the fridge and pulled out a carton of milk.

"How'd you sleep, Perry?" he asked.

"Good," I said. I'd barely slept at all but I wasn't about to tell him about my nightmares. I got out a cereal bowl and the box of Raisin Bran.

"I'm thinking you've learned your lesson," said Dad. "Let's be done with this grounding business."

I dumped cereal into the bowl. I had to fight down the thick wad of feelings that all of a sudden poured into my head and made it pound. "Are you serious?" I asked. I bit my lower lip. Three whole weeks of being a prisoner.

"Yeah," said Dad. "Maybe I overdid it a bit."

"Maybe," I said. I'd tried to pretend being grounded was no big deal. Now it was over. My eyes were stinging, but I didn't dare rub them.

"What'd your mom have to say?" asked Dad. He might as well have thrown a bomb at me.

"Huh?" I fumbled the spoon in my hand and it clattered to the floor. I picked it up.

"In the letter I brought you yesterday." I could feel his eyes on me. I sat on a stool at the counter and poured milk on top of the cereal.

"Nothing," I said, making my hand pour without shaking. "Same old stuff." I concentrated on eating. The rough flakes scratched my tongue. The raisins stuck in my teeth. I wasn't hungry at all.

"Maybe you should go see her." A mouthful of cereal stuck in my throat. I tried to swallow it three times before it went down. I felt like puking.

"No!" I sputtered. "I don't want to see her."

"I should've sent you down a long time ago," he said. "It's not right—"

"*NO!*" I interrupted. I didn't want to hear any more. I forced my voice to be calmer. "No way. I *really* don't need to see her, okay? I don't even miss her. Really."

"You sure? It's up to you."

"Yeah," I said. "I'm sure." I picked up the sugar bowl and dumped a load of sugar on my cereal. Out of the corner of my eye I saw Dad stand up. He took his coffee cup to the sink and rinsed it out. After he shut off the water he stood there for a minute looking out. The silence was so thick it felt like I was smothering in Jell-O. Finally I had to say something. "Can I go out today?"

"Sure," said Dad, still looking out. "You're not grounded anymore." His voice was tired now, and quiet.

"I'd like to go to the cave," I said. "If you don't mind."

"Sure. Draw me a map so I'll know how to find you if I need to."

"Fine." I said. I gulped down my cereal while Dad stared out the window. I couldn't wait to get out of there, but there was something I was dying to ask him. I already had an awful case of indigestion and no wonder. I drank the last of the milk, wiped my mouth, and slid off the stool. My heart raced. I grabbed the edge of the table—for support, I guess. "How come you never asked me before?"

"Asked you what?"

"About going to see Mom?"

Dad turned around slowly to face me. "When she left," he said, "it gave me full custody until the divorce was worked out. She only filed for divorce last year. I don't know why it took her so long." He looked at his hands, like he was looking for specks of dirt or something. I held my breath, waiting for him to tell me more, wishing I had never asked in the first place. Dad sighed. "I told her not to call, not to put pressure on you. That's why she only writes. She let me have full custody after the divorce. And . . . ," he paused and took a deep breath, "I didn't want you to see her. I could have sent you down."

"It's okay," I said, way, way too quickly. My voice squeaked a little. "I never wanted to see her. Still don't. Honest. Not after what happened and everything."

"I thought it would be better to make a clean break," said Dad, more to himself than to me. "Maybe that wasn't right. Maybe it was pure selfishness." He looked at my face now. His words dangled in the air between us as we stared at each other for a few seconds. I noticed the gray hair above Dad's ears, the creases in his skin around his eyes and mouth. He looked way, way older than thirty-six.

"It doesn't matter," I said.

"I should have told you all this sooner," said Dad.

I shook my head but he didn't see me.

"I'm not good at, uh . . ." His words trailed off for what felt like forever. "I'm not good at . . . talking."

"No problem, Dad," I said, making my voice cheerful even though I felt like choking. I had to get out of there. I didn't want to hear any more. "I don't miss Mom at all," I said. "Her letters are really dumb. I'm going to the cave now, okay?"

Dad nodded.

I spun around and hurried to my room to change. As I tugged on my thickest pair of wool socks, I heard the truck pull away from the house. I shut off all the thoughts that tried to invade my brain right then, about my mom, about what Dad had said about visiting her, and all the other stuff that came after that. Instead, I had this big debate with myself before I could get up the nerve to call the Pestalozzi house.

I was dying to call, to tell them I wasn't grounded anymore, but I was scared. It had been pretty rude of me to lie to Willow. She'd only been trying to cheer me up. I felt like a real slime about that. Maybe she wouldn't even want to talk to me. Guess

I couldn't blame her. Still, there was this urge in me to call. I wanted to *see* somebody, to see Willow and all of them. I had to do something so I wouldn't think about what Dad had said. It felt like I'd been away for a hundred years. Finally I punched in the numbers.

The Pestalozzis must have been at church or something, because I got the answering machine. I almost hung up. I hate those machines. After taking such a long time to decide to call, talking to a machine was not what I had in mind. But when it beeped, I took a deep breath and left a message. "This is Perry, Willow," I said. "I'm not grounded anymore and I'm going to the cave right now, so, maybe I'll see you around." Maybe she wouldn't get it until later, I thought. Maybe they forgot to check for messages every time. It's no big deal. I got along fine all that time before Willow came, didn't I?

That's what I told myself all the way to the cave. It was slow going, with at least three feet of snow on the ground now. Even with my snowshoes it took twice as long as usual to get there. The trail was indistinguishable, but I'd know my way blind. Rhonda bounded through the drifts like a puppy, burrowing under the snow and popping out covered with white. I was probably a hundred yards away when I smelled the smoke, and fifty when I saw the thin curl of white spiraling up from beyond the granite hill, where my cave was. I hurried as best as I could the rest of the way.

"Hey!" I yelled as soon as I was close enough for her to hear me. Sweat poured from my face and burned my eyes but I didn't care. It had to be her in there. It could only be her.

"Perry!" came a voice from inside the cave, and Willow's head popped out. She grinned. I felt my own face break into a grin too. "Oh, hurry! *Hurry!*" she yelled. "I have the coolest surprise for you!" She ducked back inside. I unstrapped my snowshoes and leaned them against the rock. I couldn't wait to get inside.

CHAPTER
20

Willow had already dug out the snow around the entrance. I squeezed inside. She was standing beside the fire with a long black thing in her arms. After being out in the bright snow, I could hardly see. Willow jumped up and down a little. She was smiling ear to ear, I could tell that much, and her glasses had slipped way down. "What do you think?" she asked.

"Is that the cool surprise?" I asked. I squinted to see what the black thing was. It was as big around as a large coffee can and about three feet long. There was a curly red ribbon tied around the middle and about sixty of those stick-on bows pasted all over it. Willow held it out to me.

"Don't you get it?" she said. "Don't you know what it is? Ooooooh," she exclaimed, "here, take it." I took the thing from her and instantly recognized what I was holding.

"It's a piece of stovepipe," I said. "Covered with bows."

"That's just *part* of the surprise, silly," she said, pushing up her glasses. "Don't you love it?"

I have to admit I was feeling slightly dense. She must have figured it out by the look on my face.

"Of course it's part of a stovepipe," she said, grinning like an ape. "But, see, it's from a *stove*! It was out in the little barn, the shed thingie, the place my dad is making into an art studio. It's a stove! A whole stove! Dad doesn't want it. He says it'll dry out his canvases and paints and stuff too much. We can put it in the cave and it'll stay warm *all winter*!" Willow hugged herself and jumped in circles, her ponytail flying out from her head. "I can come here and draw, and you can sit by the fire, and we can listen for wolves, and . . . oh . . . it's a little teeny potbelly stove. It's *adorable*! Aren't you happy? Merry Christmas!"

A bright light went on in my brain. A woodstove! For the cave! I quickly eyeballed the cave entrance. If the stove was small enough, we could get it in at the bottom, where the opening was the widest. No problem! A woodstove would keep it way warmer than a fire, and it wouldn't smoke up the ceiling. I could come every day if I wanted. I could get a lantern and bring my schoolwork here. For a second I remembered all those days of getting up late and lying around the house, avoiding Dad, not doing my schoolwork, feeling like a slug. I put those thoughts out of my head. It was such a great feeling to be here and to see Willow and to have that stovepipe in my hand, that I practically hopped around like Willow was doing. Instead, I started calculating. Where should we put the stove? Where would the pipe go out?

Willow grabbed my arm. "There's only one problem."

"What's that?"

"We have to show my dad the cave. So he can bring up the stove and help us put it together."

I thought about her words. The location of the cave wouldn't be a secret anymore. It had been my hideaway, my secret place for a long time. I'd spent a lot of hours there, sitting, thinking, learning bird songs. It had been all mine up until Willow came, and even afterward, I'd still thought of it as mine.

The stovepipe section was heavy in my arms. I

held one end of it up to my face and looked down the long sooty tube at Willow.

"I don't think we can move it ourselves, Perry," she said.

"I don't care if we tell him," I said through the pipe. I had the strangest feeling of relief when I said that. I wanted to hop around too, but I would have looked like a dork, so instead I pulled off a bow and stuck it to my head. "Let's tell your sisters too. Let's tell everyone." Willow put her hands on her hips and looked at me sideways.

"Are you sick?" she asked. "You're the one who wanted it to be all top secret. You made me promise I wouldn't tell anyone."

"Things change," I said, sticking another bow on my head. "We can make it a clubhouse, make rules about who can come and when, you know? It'll still be the coolest place in the woods."

"That's for sure," said Willow. Then she giggled. "Hey, give me a bow." I handed her a bow and she stuck it to the top of her head. "This can be our club hat."

"Nice hat," I said. I bobbed my head back and forth, and one of my bows flew off.

"I'll be the president," said Willow.

"No way," I said.

"Yeah, because I provided the stove."

"Okay," I said, "but I'm the CEO."

"What's a CEO?" Willow asked.

"Chief executive officer," I said. "That means I have all the power."

"Okay, Mr. Power. You can be in charge of carrying all the firewood forever," said Willow.

"Not likely," I said, but I smiled when I said it.

"I can't wait to tell my sisters," said Willow. "In order to become members of the Cave Club," she said in a deep voice, "you will have to wear the Cave Club hat to school for a whole day." Willow giggled.

"And also," I continued in an even lower voice, "you will have to wear it to bed and in the bathtub." Willow stuck bows on both her cheeks. We laughed until she started to dig in her backpack.

"I brought some snacks," said Willow.

"*Noooo!*" I said, faking surprise. That made her start laughing again. We ate M&M's and drank two cans of Coke apiece. Willow belched really loud and pretty soon we were having a burping contest, but burping and cracking up don't go too well together. Finally, my stomach hurt like crazy from belching and laughing.

"I love laughing," said Willow, and she snorted a couple times until I threatened to eat the rest of the M&M's. When we were finally quiet, all we could hear was our own breathing and the cracking and popping of the campfire, which had begun to die down. Willow picked up the stovepipe and pointed it at me. She put her face to it and looked through. "I'm glad you're not grounded anymore," she said.

I grabbed the other end and looked through at that goofy, happy face. "Me too."

Later, we went down the hill to Willow's house. The whole place was decorated for Christmas, even the yard. There were these three wooden reindeer stuck in the snow and a wreath on the door. Inside, their tree was huge. It took up half the living room. Something good was cooking, something spicy. Willow said it was cinnamon rolls. The house smelled like a holiday.

Willow showed me the potbelly stove in the shed. It was so small! Just like the kind in Western movies. I couldn't wait to have it in the cave. Mr. Pestalozzi said he'd be glad to put it in, whenever we wanted. School was out, any day would be fine. Willow said, "How about the day of Christmas Eve?"

And I said OK, even though secretly, I would have liked to have done it right then and there. It was a great Christmas present, the best I'd ever gotten.

I called Dad around four and he said it was OK for me to stay for dinner. He said thanks for calling him, too. Ian sat on my lap the whole time. Mrs. Pestalozzi offered to put him in the highchair. I said he wasn't hurting anything. He got pizza all over my sweatshirt, but it's an old one. After dinner, Mrs. Pestalozzi took him upstairs for his bath and Willow got out the Monopoly board. Cara and Alison started fighting about the dog. I took the thimble.

We ate cinnamon rolls and drank hot chocolate and played Monopoly. Mrs. Pestalozzi gave me a five-hundred-dollar bonus because she said she'd missed me so much. I got to foreclose on Alison twice. She stuck her tongue out at me the second time and I poked her under the armpit, which made her squeal and made everyone else laugh. Cara made popcorn twice. All evening long, I didn't think once about my mom or my dad or divorces or being grounded. All of that was a million miles away.

After two hours or so, I had hotels on every side. I'd never felt so rich in my life.

CHAPTER
21

The next five days flew by. I spent most of my time at the Pestalozzis'. It feels terrible to say it, but I didn't want to be around my dad. Whenever I was with him, even if we weren't talking about anything, I started thinking about what he'd said about visiting Mom. I didn't want to think about her, not even for three seconds. And Dad seemed even quieter than ever before, if that's possible. Being around him and not talking made me feel like there was something important I should do or say but I couldn't figure out what. Hanging out at Willow's at least gave me some time to forget about my own house feeling so weird.

It turned out the old stove needed a lot of cleaning and fixing. First, we had to take it all apart and get it out of the shed. That took a couple days because we had to take out the chimney and fix up the hole it left in the roof. We found three pieces of extra stovepipe up in the rafters of the shed and an elbow joint. After we got it all disassembled, Mr. P and Willow and I hauled the little stove down to their basement and we sanded off the rusty spots and painted the whole thing with black stove paint. Each coat of paint had to dry twenty-four hours. Then we greased the hinges and made sure all the moving parts moved. By the twenty-third of December, the stove was in good shape, ready to put up in the cave. That night, Mr. P and Willow drove me home about eight.

"You and your dad have plans for Christmas Eve?" asked Mr. P.

I said no, none that I knew of, and immediately felt a ton of guilt. Getting the stove ready and everything, I hadn't thought much about Christmas. Dad hadn't mentioned it. We didn't have a tree, but that was no surprise. We hadn't had one the year before either. "Cutting down a perfectly good tree is a waste," he'd said. Now it was almost Christmas again. The Pestalozzis were giving me the stove, even though Willow and the other girls would get to use it too. I didn't have anything to give them. Nothing. And I didn't have a present for my dad.

"Why don't you come to our house for dinner tomorrow night," said Mr. P. "And bring your dad."

"We're having turkey," said Willow. She turned all the way around in her seat and grinned at me. "Gobble, gobble, gobble."

"I'll ask," I said, still thinking about presents.

"You can let me know tomorrow, when we take the stove up the hill, okay?" said Mr. P.

"Okay. What time should I come? To help with the stove?"

"How about nine?" said Willow.

"That's fine with me," said her dad. "It may take several trips up and down, and besides, I need a couple of guides to this secret cave before I can do anything."

"Okay," I said. "I'll see you then." Mr. P pulled the car into our driveway and stopped. I climbed out and said thanks.

"Don't forget to ask your dad," said Willow.

"I won't," I said. I didn't tell them that he'd probably say no, like he did at Thanksgiving. I waved, shut the car door, and ran up the stairs, two at a time. Rhonda greeted me on the porch. I stooped over to pet her, and when I stood back up I could see through the window on the front door. Inside, a Christmas tree took up nearly half our living room.

When I opened the door I could see Dad kneeling next to three paper grocery bags on the floor by the Christmas tree. He pulled a new box of tree lights out of one bag. "Hey, just in time," he said. "Want to give me a hand with this?" He nodded up at the tree. It was an enormous tree, a spruce. Its smell filled our house.

"Sure," I said, feeling just a little funny inside, excited, squirmy, confused. What about wasting trees? I took off my jacket and boots and went over by Dad. "What're in the bags?"

"Ornaments, lights, tinsel," he said. "I drove into town today." He handed me another box of lights. "Lights go on first, right?"

"Right," I said, opening the box and unwinding the pointed little lights from their packaging. I had about half of them undone when Dad spoke again.

"Your mom was always in charge of the tree," he said. "Remember?"

I didn't say anything. I just kept unwinding. I took my time. I counted the little lights. *Blue, yellow, green, red, white, orange, blue.* Rhonda whined out on the porch. I set the lights down and hurried to let her in. I got the whole string of lights up before Dad said anything else.

"I went by the post office," said Dad. "There's a card for you over on the counter."

"Thanks," I said. I pulled a chair over to the tree and started stringing a second batch of lights.

"I think it's from your mom," said Dad. He had a box of gold glass balls in his hands. He was putting little metal hooks through the tops of them. He didn't look at me.

"Yeah, okay," I said, concentrating on untangling two lights that were stuck.

"Don't you want to open it?"

"What?" I hooked the end of the lights up on the highest twig.

"The card. It's a big one."

"Not right now," I said. I reached behind the tree, draping the lights carefully, staring at the tree branches, wishing I could get away, but wanting to stay and help. I wanted to change the subject in a desperate way. I tried a distraction tactic. "The Pestalozzis want us to come for dinner tomorrow night," I said. There. I'd asked him. I knew he'd say no, but at least he would stop talking about *her*.

"What time?"

I stopped and looked down at him. "You want to go?"

"Sure. Then I don't have to cook Christmas dinner."

Last year we'd had spaghetti, not like it's any big deal to fix. I was stunned. "Uh, they usually eat around five-thirty," I said. "We're putting a stove in the cave tomorrow."

"A stove?" said Dad. I hadn't told him a single thing about it. Now I felt sort of bad, but jeez, when had I had a chance? He'd been giving me the silent treatment for days.

"A potbelly woodstove. So we can hang out in the cave even when it gets really cold."

"You got wood?" asked Dad.

"A little," I said. "I used a lot of it that night I was, uh, in there."

Dad nodded and stood up. He hung one of the gold balls right next to my head. "Five-thirty?"

"Yeah."

"Do I have to dress up?"

I felt a smile creep up my cheeks. "No, Dad. They aren't a dressing-up family."

Dad really went overboard when he bought all the

decorations. By the time we were done, the tree was practically hidden from sight under all the balls and tinsel and plastic reindeer and snowmen. I plugged in the tree lights. One of the strings blinked. Dad lit a fire and we turned off all the house lights. For about an hour we just sat there, me on the floor, Dad in a chair by the fire, hanging around and not saying anything, but it wasn't like I wanted to talk and I didn't have that itchy feeling because Dad wasn't talking. Being quiet like that, with the tree lit up, was perfect. Rhonda leaned up against me and pretty soon my eyes were heavy. Christmas trees are so cool, I thought lazily. Especially when they're full of presents—that thought jolted me awake. Christmas presents! For sure Dad would give me presents. He always did, even when we didn't have a tree. I still didn't have any presents for him, or for anyone else.

I scrambled up from the floor. "I'm dying of tiredness, Dad," I said and yawned a big fake one. "Time to hit the sack."

"Okay," said Dad. He was staring into the fire. "Do you like the tree?"

"Yeah," I said, wanting all of a sudden to hug him like Willow and her sisters were always hugging their dad. I knew he wouldn't like it, though, because he isn't the hugging type, so I hurried off to my room to make Christmas presents. I pulled the finished deerskin out from under my bed and got out my leather tools.

My clock radio read 2:17 when I finished. My fingers ached. My eyes were blurry. I'd had just enough leather, just enough waxed thread. Poking all the holes with the awl had been the hardest part, that and cutting the really skinny pieces. It felt good to be finished. It felt great to have presents for everyone.

Even with my door shut I could smell the Christmas tree. The smell made me feel good too. OK, I told myself. One more trip to the bathroom and I can collapse into bed. I made my way silently down the hall to the bathroom, breathing in the delicious spruce smell all the way. I didn't turn on the light until I was inside and the door was shut. I reached for my toothbrush and saw something that made my stomach grab my whole body in a paralyzing twist-hold.

It was my dad's old leather Day-Timer date book flopped open next to the sink. On one side was a calendar page, on the other, a tiny tablet of blank

notepaper, only it wasn't blank. Dad had written TO
DO at the top. Underneath those words, there was a
list.

> —*call Dobbs re: broken chain saw*
> —*gas*
> —*mail*
> —*delivery to Matanens', Dec. 23rd:12 cords*

It wasn't any of those regular things that got my
attention. It was the last thing on the list, the one
that made my heart beat like I'd just run the
marathon, the one that I knew would keep me from
sleeping all night, no matter how dead tired I felt. I
stared at that list. I stared at the last thing Dad had
written.

> —*call Jennie*

CHAPTER
22

No way could I sleep after seeing that list. Why did Dad want to call Mom? Why, after all this time? Or had he called her before and I just never knew about it? Why would he call her if her lawyer was the one who kept in touch with him? Why did he want to talk to Mom? After everything that had happened, why now?

I must have asked myself those same questions a million times before the first gray light of dawn crept into my room around seven-thirty and Rhonda started whining to be let out. My head ached. My eyeballs felt like they were full of sand. My mouth was sticky and my tongue felt about two times normal size. I wanted to sleep, I HAD to sleep, but I couldn't. It's like my brain was all revved up in high gear even though my body was exhausted. All I could think of was that list, my mom's name and my dad calling her on the phone after almost three years' time.

Had he already called? Had they talked?

I was too tired to think about it, too tired not to think about it. At eight the phone rang and I rolled out of bed. I let Rhonda out and heard the phone ring again. Dad picked it up. He listened and then checked his watch.

"Sure, I can get it to you today," he said. I crept back to my room and dressed myself. I had to eat. I had to get to the Pestalozzis' by nine. I had to stop thinking about *it*. I reminded myself of all the good stuff, like that we were putting in the stove and that it was Christmas Eve and that I had presents for everyone, and like that Dad was going to come with me to the Pestalozzis' for dinner. So what if he called my mom? I mean, I wasn't SURE he'd never called her before. Maybe he called her every Christmas to tell her how tall I was or how my schoolwork was coming along, something like that. Maybe the divorce judge had said he *had* to call her once a year. Judges can make divorced people do all kinds of things, can't they? Dad's phone calls weren't any of my business.

After I was dressed, I went down to get myself

some breakfast. "I've got a delivery in Duluth today," said Dad.

"*Duluth?*" I said. Duluth is really far from here, more than a hundred miles. "That's far."

"This guy says he can't get a decent price on hardwood anywhere around there," said Dad. "He's willing to pay for the extra distance." My heart sank down to my knees. I couldn't help Dad with a load, not today. Not on the day we were going to put in the stove. Not on the day my poor body was so pooped I could barely lift a spoon to my mouth.

"You go on and help put that stove in," Dad said. "I can do this one alone." I fought back the urge to let out a humongous sigh of relief.

"You sure?" I asked.

"Sure. I'll be back by three or four."

At twenty to nine Dad was out loading the truck. I strapped on my snowshoes. The Christmas presents were in my pockets. The sky was heavy with dark clouds that looked like the underside of a bunch of fat gray geese. The air was still and cold and it felt like snow. Rhonda barked impatiently at me and trotted off down the trail we'd made over the last few days.

The cold air woke me up some, but my legs and

arms felt weak and it took me longer than usual to get to Willow's house. At the ledge where the cave is, I had to stop and get my breath for a long time before I was ready to go down the long steep hill. Going without sleep is not a cool feeling. It was going to be a long, long day.

It took us four trips to get the stove and all the pipes and chimney stuff up the hill. The stove itself was way too heavy for one person to carry, so Mr. P laid it down on one of those metal flying saucers and pulled the whole thing up the hill while the rest of us pushed. I say "the rest of us" meaning me and Willow doing all the work, and the little sisters tagging along and getting in the way. At first, Mrs. Pestalozzi wasn't going to let Katie come because she had a cold, but Katie begged and blubbered until the grownups gave in. She stuck to me like a shadow the whole time, sniffling her head off. I was too tired to be bugged.

When Mr. P and Willow's sisters saw the cave for the first time, they were impressed, I could tell, especially by all the drawings. On the one hand, it felt very weird to have so many people in my cave. On the other hand, it felt cool for them to share in it.

Mr. P said my drawings were excellent. Alison found Willow's sketchbook but Willow grabbed it out of her hands before she could open it. "Those are my private drawings," she said. Alison stuck out her tongue.

Cara said maybe I would grow up to be an artist like her dad. Mr. P said he'd actually seen cave drawings on a trip to France when he was in college. He even knew, just by looking, which caves I'd copied some of them from. That made me feel good.

We worked all morning to get the stove stuff up the hill and laid out in the order it had to go in. We put the stove near the entrance, but not so near that all the heat would go out. Then we had to put the stovepipe up and put the elbow joints together in such a way that the smoke would go out at the top of the entrance, like it did before. Mr. P had brought some tools. It was really neat how he drilled right into solid rock and set the supports for the stovepipe.

Finally, the whole thing was hooked up. "Good job, guys," said Mr. P. He smiled and that big space in his teeth showed. He explained how to open the damper, how to light the stove, how to make sure the chimney was drawing the smoke out, and he gave us a long safety lecture. When he was done, we all stood around and stared at the stove like it was some sacred object. For a minute, everyone was silent.

"We have to test it!" Willow burst out, so she and her sisters scrambled to get firewood and matches. They chattered a mile a minute as they stacked the kindling tepee style and fought about which piece should go where. Finally, Willow took the box of matches from Cara and was just about to strike one when she turned around and handed it to me.

"You should light the stove, Perry Dubwah," she said. "It was your cave first." I struck the match and held it under the dry kindling. At first I wasn't sure it would light. Then a small splinter caught, and another one, and then one side of the piece of wood, and then the whole piece lit up. The flames licked the other wood and all the kindling caught fire.

"Yahoo!" yelled Willow. She grabbed me by the shoulders and hopped up and down.

Alison and Cara and Katie held hands and did Ring-Around-the-Rosy, chanting, "The stove, the stove, the STO-O-O-VE!" until Cara squealed.

"Katie! You are so gross!" she yelled. "Dad, she

has boogers all over her hands!" Cara rubbed her own hand on her jacket. "Why don't you use a Kleenex once in a while?" she demanded.

Katie dug under her snow pants and pulled out a ball of used Kleenex.

"It's all squished," she said. "See, Dad?"

Mr. P nodded absent-mindedly and checked the chimney to make sure the smoke was going out like it was supposed to.

"Looks perfect," he said and clapped me on the shoulder with one hand. "Thanks for sharing your hideout with the kids," he said quietly. "It means a lot to them."

I nodded.

"And to me too," he added. All of a sudden I felt warm all over. It must have been from the stove, which was now cranking out the heat full blast. It had begun to snow hard outside, and the wind was blowing from the north. It didn't matter, though. Not with the stove going. We poked some bigger pieces of wood in the door and shut it tight.

"Snacks?" asked Willow, holding up her ever-present backpack, and we settled down to feed our faces.

About half an hour later, Katie had to go to the

bathroom, and as soon as she said it, everyone else had to go too, me included. Mr. P showed us how to shut all the vents and the damper to make the fire smother itself. "You don't want to put dirt or water in here," he said. "That would ruin the stove. If you shut out all the air, the fire will go out quickly"— he did it as he talked— "and the wood that's left in there will be good the next time."

"You should *never* waste wood," Alison said in a know-it-all way.

Thinking of wasting wood reminded me of our Christmas tree, which reminded me of staying up all night, which made me yawn. I felt happy about the stove, really, but I was so tired it was hard to feel totally thrilled. It was hard to feel anything, except my back, which ached, and my head, which pounded, and my arms and legs that felt like noodles, and my stomach, which felt shriveled up because I was starving in spite of all the snacks. I thought about the evening to come and that revived me some. Turkey dinner. My mouth watered just thinking about it. And Dad would be there.

On the way down to Willow's house, I felt my coat pockets a couple times. The presents were safe and sound. If I could just stop thinking about seeing my mom's name on that list, everything would be perfect. *It could be some other person named Jennie,* I thought suddenly. *It could be somebody who needs wood.* Why hadn't I thought of that before? There must be millions of Jennies in America! I grabbed a handful of snow and made a ball and lobbed it right at Willow's back. It broke apart on her coat with a splat.

"Hey!" she yelled, twirling around. "You big turkey!" She scooped up some snow and threw it at me. She missed me by a mile.

CHAPTER
23

By five it was pitch dark outside and snowing hard. And there was no sign of Dad. I called home a couple times and got the machine. I wanted to sit by a window and watch for him, but I was too embarrassed. Where was he? Was he still in Duluth? Had he forgotten about dinner? I checked on Rhonda a couple times. Mr. P had put her in the garage with the other dogs so she'd be out of the snow during dinner. Both times I went out to the garage, I stood and looked down the road, listening for Dad, but he didn't come.

Willow and her sisters decided to watch that old movie *It's a Wonderful Life*. I lay down on the carpet in the living room next to Willow, and Ian came and sat on me like I was a horse. After a while he got up, found a blanket and a blue pacifier, and came and lay down beside me on the other side. I turned to look at him. His nose was almost touching mine. He had Cheerios breath. I made a face at him. "Hey, cereal breath," I said. He frowned.

"No, no. Shhhh, Berry," he said around the pacifier. "Night-night." He squinted his eyes at me. I almost cracked up, but I did what he wanted. I shut my eyes and pretended to go to sleep. I felt a little hand on my cheek. Ian patted me gently. "Night-night," he said. He kept patting me. He was cute, but right then I wished he'd go away. I almost got up but I was tired, dead, dead tired, and the carpet was soft. I heard Willow tell Cara to quit blocking the TV. My eyes felt glued shut. Ian patted me a few more times and then he quit. I heard him get up and toddle off. I let out a big sigh and fell asleep.

I don't know how long I slept. I heard Mrs. Pestalozzi call, "Dinner! Merry Christmas, everyone!" and I opened my eyes. The movie was still playing, but I could tell it was almost over. It took me a minute to get moving. I felt like a real deadhead. The girls switched off the TV and found a radio station playing Christmas music.

"We can watch the ending of the movie later," said Willow. I dragged myself off the floor. Where was Dad? How could we eat without him?

"Did my dad call or anything?" I asked Mr. P when I got to the table.

"No, Perry," he said sadly. "And it's snowing really hard out. I doubt if he'll make it back, so we'll go ahead and eat. Dinner has been ready for more than an hour. We may get fifteen to twenty inches tonight."

"He'll make it," I said, trying to sound sure of myself. "He's got the blade on the truck."

"Some sections of the highway are closed," said Mr. P. "We'll save some food for your dad, just in case."

"You can stay with us, Perry," said Willow. She pushed her glasses into place and blew a long strand of dark hair out of her face. "We can pretend you're part of our family, like a cousin or a brother or something." She grinned and wiggled her eyebrows up and down.

"Yeah," said Cara. "I'd like a big brother WAY better than two big sisters."

"What's wrong with big sisters?" asked Alison. "Huh? Little sisters are a real pain in the butt, not big sisters."

"I'm not a pain in the butt," said Cara.

"Mom," said Katie, "Cara and Alison said butt!"

"*Girls,*" said Mr. P.

"Who wants turkey?" asked Mrs. Pestalozzi, carrying a big tray in and setting it down on the table. Dad was supposed to be here. He'd promised. I'd told them he was coming.

"I'm starved," I said in a fakey cheerful voice.

There was turkey, dressing, mashed potatoes, sweet potatoes, green beans, cinnamon rolls, cranberry sauce, corn, lots of gravy, and the biggest bowl of olives I'd ever seen. I ate and ate, forcing myself to enjoy the food, forcing myself not to think about Dad. I felt angry and worried at the same time and kept telling myself it was stupid to feel that way. It wasn't his fault he'd been caught in a storm. So why was I upset? I was still dead tired, even after taking a nap; in fact, I was so tired it felt like work to chew. The food tasted good in my mouth, but as soon as it hit my stomach it made me feel gross. I watched Mr. P cut up the turkey into chunks for Ian. How come Willow got a dad who didn't go out on jobs? It wasn't fair. The wind howled outside and rattled the windows. I ate without talking at all. My jaws were too tired to do both.

After dinner Willow and Mr. P cleared the plates

and brought out two apple pies and a gallon of ice cream. I was stuffed, but the ice cream looked good. They scooped and sliced and soon everyone had a plate of pie and ice cream. Mr. P sat down and I was just about to dive into the ice cream when he clinked his fork against his water glass.

"Attention, attention," he said. "Mom and I have an announcement to make. A little family Christmas present." He looked over at Mrs. Pestalozzi and smiled. She grinned back at him, winked one eye, and blew a strand of hair out of her face, just like Willow had done before dinner. "Sometime around the Fourth of July," he said, "there's going to be another little Pestalozzi around this place."

For about two seconds no one made a sound. Then Katie jumped up in her chair and started to dance around. "A baby sister! A little sister!" Then she sneezed and sprayed the table with ice cream drops.

"Sick, Katie," said Alison. "Why don't you cover up? You are so disgusting."

"That's it, no more sisters!" said Willow. "Another brother!" She slid out of her seat and hugged her mom. "Oh, Mom, another sister is okay, I guess." Mrs. Pestalozzi put her arm around Willow and kissed her cheek.

Alison got out of her chair. "I'll share my room with the new baby," she said, "instead of with Cara." Cara stuck out her tongue at Alison.

"We don't have to worry about bedrooms tonight," said Mrs. Pestalozzi.

"I don't want to sleep with Ian no more," said Katie from her chair. "He snorts."

Mr. P looked at me and rolled his eyes. He was smiling so hard his cheeks looked like they hurt. I tried to smile back at him, but it was a lousy attempt. How could they be so excited about another baby? Weren't five kids enough? I poked my ice cream around with my fork.

"Isn't that great, Perry Dubwah?" asked Willow. "Yippee! The Pestalozzis are taking over Minnesota!" Everyone laughed at her comment, everyone but me. I only smiled.

Pretty soon Ian got into the mood of things, banging his spoon on his highchair tray. Willow's sisters stopped bickering and for a couple minutes the whole dining room was one big mass of happy family sounds. Finally, everyone settled down and started eating. Willow leaned across the table. She pointed her spoon in my direction.

"Wouldn't it be cool if the baby was born on the

actual Fourth of July?" Some ice cream dripped out of her mouth. She licked it off her chin. "I mean, we could call him Boom Boom!" She giggled and snorted, which made everyone else laugh again, everyone but me, that is.

"You sound like a pig when you do that, Willow," said Alison.

"At least I'm a happy pig," said Willow, and she snorted again. "Not crabby like *you*."

"That's enough, girls," said Mrs. Pestalozzi, but she was smiling when she said it.

My stomach hurt from wondering about my dad. Now I felt weird on top of it, totally out of place in the middle of this loud family that could never decide whether to fight or celebrate. Now they were celebrating and the commotion was incredible. What was the big deal about having another baby? A lady sang on the radio.

I'll be home for Christmas
You can plan on me . . .

I felt someone touch my elbow. It was Katie. She leaned up against me and patted my arm. I hoped it wasn't the same hand she wiped her nose with. "Poor old Perry Dubwah," she said. "'Cuz you're a only child."

Her words were like a slap in the face. All of a sudden I felt wide awake, aware of every sound, including my own breathing, which seemed extra loud right then.

Please have snow and mistletoe . . .

Everyone stopped talking and looked at me. I wanted to slide under the table. Katie kept patting my arm. *Pat, pat, pat.* I wanted to yell at her, push her away. Something inside me was growing, filling me up, pushing to get out. I stared at my ice cream and swallowed.

"Not everyone has a big family, Katie," said Mrs. Pestalozzi. "It's just fine that Perry is an only child." Her voice was warm and kind. An only child.

And presents on the tree . . .

I felt her eyes on me. I felt all their eyes on me. Then I heard myself start talking.

"I'm not an only child." My voice sounded small, far away, like it was coming from another person.

"You never told me you had any—," started Willow, but that little voice that was mine but not mine interrupted her.

"I had a sister," I said. Ian stopped banging his spoon.

Christmas Eve will find me . . .

The sink dripped in the kitchen. They watched me and they breathed so loud I could hear them, and my heart went a million miles an hour. "My sister figured out how to unbuckle the car seat," I said. "She climbed over into the front." My voice felt scratchy, croaky, like a frog's. "My mom should have stopped, should have buckled my sister in."

Where the love-light gleams . . .

"A truck hit them from behind." The music was so loud it hurt my ears. "My sister went through the windshield." My voice squeaked on the last word. It was like my mouth had taken over my whole head, saying things I didn't want it to say. The words had tumbled past my teeth and into the air for everyone to hear. I couldn't stop them. All of a sudden my throat felt like someone was squeezing it. I could hardly breathe.

I'll be home for Christmas . . .
If only in my dreams.

"After that, my mom left."

I stared hard at the white shiny lump of melting ice cream until it turned into a blur. I blinked and blinked to clear my vision, but the ice cream stayed blurred. The song was over. The disc jockey announced the next Christmas song. The sound of my heartbeat filled up my head and throbbed in my ears. I bit my lip until I tasted blood. One tear spilled over from my eye and ran down my cheek. I couldn't move to wipe it. I was paralyzed. I could only stare at that blurry ice cream. Stare and blink. Stare and blink.

An arm went around behind my back and someone strong hugged me. Willow's dad. Chair legs scraped against the floor and then two hands rested on my shoulders and squeezed. Someone kissed me on the top of my head and I saw a streak of long red hair as it swept past my cheek. "We're sorry, honey," whispered Mrs. Pestalozzi. Willow slid out of her chair and came around to me. So did Alison and Cara. Katie patted my leg. Ian banged on his tray.

I felt Willow's face lean in toward me. "We had no idea, Perry Dubwah," she whispered.

I was surrounded by Pestalozzis, touching me, breathing on me. Something inside popped. Something let go. At first I just shook all over, like there was an earthquake inside my body.

I put my head down on the table and bawled until I thought I would explode.

CHAPTER
24

Huge sobs shook me. I felt like an idiot but I couldn't stop. I tried to be quiet, but my breath came in with big gulps. I cried about moving, about missing Grandma, about not having any friends for such a long, long time. I cried about my dad who didn't show up for Christmas Eve when he'd said he would, and I cried about my mom. She'd ruined our family forever. I cried for my sister, who loved Big Bird and called me Berry, a sister I would never, ever see again. Three years of not crying caught up to me like a tidal wave and now the awful feelings were drowning me. There was nothing I could do. I hated myself for crying like that.

Pretty soon my eyes were so swollen I could barely open them. My nose felt the size of a baseball mitt. There were so many tears that some came out my nose. I sniffled and sniffled but still they kept dripping out. The Pestalozzis didn't say a word the whole time, they just crowded around me. Part of me wanted to shove them away and run. The other part of me wanted them to come closer, wanted them to somehow smother my tears. After a while I didn't blubber anymore, but it took a lot longer for the sniffling to end.

Katie leaned against my leg. "Perry?"

I wiped my eyes and looked at her. I felt like such an idiot.

"Here's a Kleenex," she said and held that damp, awful, gooey wad of tissue right in front of my face. Her eyes were huge behind her thick red glasses. She looked so serious. I tried not to, but I just couldn't help but smile. I picked up the Kleenex by one teeny corner.

"Gee, thanks," I said, and then everyone burst out laughing, including me.

Outside, a horn sounded.

"Your dad!" yelled Willow, and she ran to the window, followed by all three of her sisters. Mr. P patted me once more on the shoulder.

"You okay now?" he asked. I nodded, wiping my nose on my sleeve. What was Dad going to think? I took a couple deep breaths. I tried to clear my brain. Mrs. Pestalozzi handed me a paper towel.

"It isn't exactly elegant, but it'll do the job." She smiled at me and I smiled back, feeling embarrassed. "Holidays can be tough when we miss someone," she said. I bet I looked like a geek, all puffy-eyed and swollen-nosed. I nodded and tried to smile anyway.

"That's neat about another baby," I said, changing the subject. My nose was completely plugged up. I blew it into the paper towel with a big honk, but it didn't help.

"Thanks, Perry," said Mrs. Pestalozzi. She grabbed my chin and shook it gently. "Now, you'd better run out and see if that's your dad."

Inside my head, a guy with a big hammer was beating away at my brain. I felt totally wiped out. I already knew it was my dad outside for sure. I'd recognized the sound of the horn. I hurried out to the front, where Willow and her dad and the other girls were standing around, looking out the open door. I saw Dad's head. He stomped the snow off his feet and stepped in.

"Nasty night to be out, eh, Jack?" said Mr. P in a

loud, friendly way. "We weren't sure you'd make it." They shook hands.

"The roads were a mess," said Dad. "I hope you didn't wait to eat." That's when he saw me. I tried to smile but my mouth wanted to turn down at the corners instead. My chin twitched.

"Hey," I said.

"What's wrong?" Dad's eyes widened. He frowned and looked hard at me. "You okay?"

I nodded. Dad's face was blurry. The Pestalozzis stood around without saying anything. I could feel Dad staring at me, examining my face, looking for clues as to why I looked like I'd just run head first into a speeding train.

"We put that stove in today," said Mr. P. "He's bushed."

"You should see the cave, Mr. Dubwah," said Willow, then her hand flew to her mouth. "Oops."

My mouth was paralyzed. My eyes burned, my nose ached. I was totally relieved to see Dad, to know he was safe, but I also felt so stupid for crying that I wished I could shrivel up and die. I couldn't say anything because my chin was twitching so bad.

"Perry told us about your daughter, Jack," said Mr. P. Dad blinked but he didn't look at Mr. P. He looked at me. All the color drained from his face. "You guys have been through a lot," said Mr. P. He put a hand on Dad's shoulder.

"Happened a long time ago," said Dad, still staring at me white-faced, ignoring the kindly hand. My stomach flopped over. Somehow I found my voice.

"I'm super tired, Dad," I said, and then I turned to Willow. "We'd better go home now, before the snow gets any deeper." I tried to smile, but it came out crooked. Willow looked quickly from me to my dad without saying anything. I grabbed my jacket from its peg and put it on. Then I remembered the presents. "Here," I said, placing seven little deer-skin leather pouches in her hands. I hadn't had time to wrap them. "These are Christmas presents for all of you. I made them. I wanted to fill yours with M&M's but I didn't have time."

Cara and Alison and Katie crowded around Willow and started talking. Willow looked over their heads at me. "You *made* these?" she mouthed in my direction. She pushed past her sisters and stood right in front of me.

"Yeah."

I pulled on my boots. Then I stood up and saw Willow holding one of the butter-soft pouches against her cheek. "Oh, thanks times a *zillion*," she squeaked. Before I had time to dodge, Willow launched herself at me, threw her arms around me, and hugged me hard. "Merry Christmas, Perry Dubwah," she whispered. "Merry Christmas."

"Hey, knock it off!" I said, struggling to get away. I was backed clean up against the wall. She quit hugging me, but her nose was only a few inches away from mine and she stood there looking as sad as Rhonda right after a bath, the little leather pouch still clutched to her cheek. Her glasses had slipped down again.

I sighed and reached over to poke Willow's glasses into place. "Okay, okay," I said. "Quit looking like that. Merry Christmas." She smiled, and I smiled back, and then it was time to go.

The road was so bad it took us almost twenty minutes to get home. Rhonda sat on the seat between us. She was like a big furry wall between me and Dad. We didn't talk at all. Dad was busy concentrating on the road, lowering the blade, plowing the snow to one side, lifting the blade, backing up, plowing down the road some more. I leaned against Rhonda and closed my eyes. Christmas songs jingled and tooted and sang in my head. Was Dad mad that I'd told the Pestalozzis about everything? I wondered it a couple times, but I was too tired to worry at all. Once I opened my eyes and realized it had quit snowing. I closed them again and buried my face in Rhonda's black fur.

Finally we got home. The front porch had huge drifts piled on it. I let Rhonda out and waited in the truck while Dad shoveled and swept the snow off. He worked hard and fast, scooping the snow, pushing it off the porch, scraping it off the porch and away from the steps. He opened the front door and motioned for me to come in. I climbed down and started up the stairs.

Suddenly I froze with my foot above the step and listened. Rhonda whined and hurried into the house. The wolf. Howling somewhere nearby.

Dad came down the stairs and stood next to me. The wolf howled again.

There was no way to tell how close or how far away it was. It could have been a mile away, it could have been a hundred yards away. The snow and darkness made it impossible to tell. Dad stood so close his jacket brushed against mine. We listened. And the wolf howled again.

I felt the hair on my neck prickle.

"Poor guy," whispered Dad. "All by himself on Christmas Eve." The wolf howled again and I shivered. Slowly, Dad reached his arm across the back of my shoulders and pulled me close. "Do you think that wolf's as lonely as we are?" he asked in a gruff whisper.

I looked up into Dad's face and saw real tears shining in his eyes. I nodded, and then I buried my face in his jacket.

The wolf howled two more times, and after that, the night was silent.

CHAPTER
25

Christmas Day I slept so late I almost forgot about the holiday. About eleven, Rhonda nosed her way into my room and started whining. When I opened my eyes, I saw she had a red bow tied around her neck. Dad must have put it there. That's when I remembered it was Christmas and hurried out to look for presents. Dad was waiting, sitting by the fire in his chair and drinking coffee. Sure enough, there were presents under the tree. "Merry Christmas, Son," he said over his cup, and he almost smiled when he said it.

Dad liked the leather pouch I made him. He said he'd probably use it for change. Dad got me a thick book about volcanoes from the National Geographic Society, some new jeans and socks, and a Swiss Army knife with a million blades and gadgets. After that we ate my favorite breakfast, waffles, and then we just hung around in the living room, staring at the tree, listening to Christmas music, reading, talking a little bit but not much. Dad asked if I wanted to learn cribbage, and I said OK. He went and dug around in his room and came out with an old cribbage board Great-grandpa Dubois had brought from Montreal. I didn't even know he had it.

A couple hours later we were playing cribbage, and I was ahead fifteen points when the phone rang. It was Willow, and she said she was just dying to tell me what everyone had gotten for Christmas and that her mom had made her wait until afternoon to call. I swear it took her half an hour just to list all the presents. Finally, I told her about my knife. She asked if it had a microwave oven on it too and hooted so loud at her own lame joke that I had to hold the phone a foot away from my head so I wouldn't go deaf. Right before we hung up, she asked if I was having a good Christmas. I told her yes.

At five-thirty, the phone rang again. Probably Willow I thought, as I crossed the room to answer it. It would be like her to forget some microscopic detail and call me back. I picked up the phone.

"Hello?" I said.

"Perry?"

It was a voice from a long time ago but I knew instantly who it was. I swallowed and felt the blood drain out of my head.

"This is Perry."

"Gosh, you sound grown up." Was there just a hint of a quiver in her voice?

"Oh. Hi." Why did my own voice sound so weird?

"Hi, yourself," she said. "How are you?"

"Good."

"I bet you're getting big." Did her voice crack on the last word?

"I guess," I answered. My ears felt cold and tingly.

"Have you gotten all my letters?"

"Yeah," I said, feeling guilty as anything.

"Maybe you could write back sometime," she said. "I'd like that. If you want."

I couldn't say anything. I'm not sure I wanted to. For sure I couldn't have, even if I'd wanted to. There was a long pause. I could hear myself breathing. I could hear her breathing too. I could feel my heart moving up into my throat, where any second it would start to choke me.

"Is your dad around? I need to talk to him."

"He's right here." I moved to give the phone to Dad but her voice stopped me.

"Perry?"

"Uh-huh?"

"I've missed you something crazy, honey." Her voice was barely above a whisper.

I knew I should say something but I couldn't get my mouth to work. I squeezed my eyes shut and swallowed.

"Merry Christmas," said my mom. "Great talking to you."

I wanted to say Merry Christmas back, at least to be polite, but I couldn't get any sound out. I handed the phone to Dad and hustled to my bedroom. I stuffed my head under my pillow so I wouldn't hear them talk. Even with the pillow over my head I couldn't keep from hearing her voice. *I've missed you something crazy, honey.*

When Dad got off the phone, I didn't want to play cribbage anymore.

We didn't talk about that phone call, not the day Mom called, not any of the days afterward. Dad didn't ask me what she'd said, and I didn't ask Dad why she'd wanted to talk to him. I had a million questions. Had he called and told her it was OK to call me on Christmas? I couldn't believe she'd have done it on her own, not after three years of no calls. She'd written all those letters, but she'd never called. Had Dad given her permission to call or something? Is that how these things work in a divorce? I wondered and thought, but Dad and I didn't talk about it. That's the way it is with us. We don't talk a lot.

I tried to forget the sound of my mom's voice on the phone but it was impossible. It was exactly like a recording in my brain that played day and night until I thought I'd go nuts. There was a war of feelings going on inside me. I wanted her to call again something awful. And I never wanted to speak to her again, not ever. How was it possible to feel both things at once? Every time the phone rang, I jumped.

The day after Christmas, Dad called the International Wolf Center in Ely to report hearing the wolf. The biologist he talked to got really excited and said they'd probably send a tracking team out in the next couple weeks. She asked Dad if we had actually seen the wolf, and he said no, but then I told him that Willow had seen it once, and he put me on the phone with the biologist. I gave her

Willow's number. She said there had been several sightings in our area and that it looked like a pair of wolves was starting a new pack. In order to keep track of the packs over time, they would have to first identify the individual wolves by sight. She said if they did a helicopter search, maybe Willow and I could go along. I told her for sure we'd want to go and she said she'd call me back. I bet I'll see King after all.

After that, we got a cold snap. The thermometer dove down to twenty-six below overnight and didn't get above zero for three days. Dad got a couple calls for wood, and once while he was out, he swung by the Pestalozzis', asked Mr. P where the cave was, and hauled up a whole bunch of wood for us. I didn't even know about it until Willow called to tell me that night. I told her about the biologist. That got her screaming. I didn't tell her about the call from my mom, though.

Then yesterday, right after breakfast, Dad made this big announcement. We were clearing off the table and he was telling me how he needed some parts for one of his chain saws, when out of the blue he said, "I think we'll head down to St. Paul on the first. What do you say?" I almost dropped the bottle of maple syrup I had in my hand. We haven't been back to St. Paul since we moved north.

"What for?" I blurted out.

"Dobbs has a buddy who fixes chain saws," he said. He set down the carton of milk on the counter and folded his arms across his chest.

"Yeah, but, way down in the Cities?"

"Maybe I'm in the mood for a long drive," said Dad.

"Do I have to go?" I asked. "I mean, sitting around while someone fixes a chain saw sounds pretty boring." My palms had gone itchy.

Dad's eyes barely crinkled at the corners. "You're a smart kid," he said. "Maybe you could think of something to do, someone you might like to visit. . . ." He turned around, put the milk in the refrigerator, and that was the end of that conversation.

I thought about going to St. Paul all day yesterday. I figured thinking about it would keep me awake all last night, but it didn't. For once, I slept like a rock. I didn't even dream. And when I woke up this morning, I knew I had something to do before we left on that trip.

IT TOOK A LOT of hard work to jam all these letters into my backpack. Three years' worth of letters is a lot. Dad didn't ask why my backpack was so stuffed when I told him I was headed to the cave, but I know he noticed it. Maybe he figured it was snacks. "Stay warm" was all he said.

The letters are out of order from being stuffed into my backpack, but the dates are on the postmarks. It makes sense to start with the oldest ones, the ones from right after we moved, the ones from way before she was Jennie Kuzak.

I don't know why, but my heart is doing double duty. It's hot in here. I must have too much wood in the stove. I feel like I'm inside a sweaty mitten. You'd never know it's ten below outside. The stove is putting out incredible heat. I'm totally pitted out.

Look at this. Here's the one I started to burn. Jennie Dubois.

Why does reading her name make my eyes water? The stove must be smoking. I'll have to check it later, right after I read this letter. I figure I can scan the rest of them in half an hour or so. She probably didn't write that much. Maybe when I'm done I'll toss them all into the stove. What a blaze that would be.

This isn't the first time I've wondered why I've

kept them for this long. They're just letters. Maybe after I read a few I'll get bored and head down the hill to see if I can get a Monopoly game going instead of reading. I wonder if the Pestalozzis came through the Twin Cities on their way from California. I'll have to ask Willow.

I unfold the smallest blade from my new pocket knife and slit open the envelope. How come my hands are shaking? It's too hot in here to be shivering. Weird.

The letter is almost three years old. I pull it out of the envelope. The paper is white with a rainbow and a couple bear stickers at the top. It's burned along one edge but I can still read all the words. It's her handwriting all right, loopy and printed big for a little second-grade kid to read. I hold the letter to my nose and take a deep breath. The paper still smells like her.

I'm ready to read it now. My eyes find the first line.

"*Dear Per Bear,*" it says. "*How's my favorite boy?*"